VIRTUE, I DEST

By
Dennis Meredith

Edited and restructured by Peter H. Dietrich

Best Wishes
Dennis Meredith
25/10/25.

Cover illustration by Alfia Kircheva

This is a work of fiction. Unless otherwise indicated, all the names, characters, businesses, places, events and incidents in this book are either the product of the author's imagination or used in a fictitious manner. Any resemblance to actual persons, living or dead, or actual events is purely coincidental.

***

First published in the United Kingdom – 2025

Copyright © Dennis Meredith – 2025
(All rights reserved)

Dennis Meredith has asserted his rights to be known as the author of this work

PART ONE - VIRTUE

Chapter One

The Mother Superior Colette, head of the 'Our Lady of Divine Mercy' children's home, was waiting for two children to come into her care from a certain Mrs. Veronica Williams. Sister Colette had a great many years of experience in looking after orphaned or abandoned children.

She had learnt from her report that Veronica Williams was addicted to alcohol, which had greatly affected her health and very soon her whole life, and that of her two young children.

Veronica had been married for twelve years with Jason Williams. When she first got married, she'd enjoyed a warm and sharing relationship with her husband, living through many happy moments together. Their happiness was greatly increased with the birth of their two daughters, Carol and Elizabeth, both charming and wonderful girls, and it seemed that the family was then complete, while Veronica felt her life to be a great gift.

But then one evening her husband had come home late from work, looking somewhat ill at ease and evasive, and after a little badgering on her part, he confessed that he'd met someone new and that he didn't love her anymore. He went on to say that he would move out of their house the following day and go to live with his new girlfriend. This was a cruel and unexpected blow in Veronica's happy family life, and she was devastated, unable to accept or believe that this could be happening to her.

When, the next day, her husband set about packing his belongings and refusing to discuss it any further with her, she realised that it was happening, and her whole world came tumbling down around her. She was thankful at least that her daughters were at school, and so they missed the dramas and had no idea of what was going on around them.

To begin with, she avoided telling the girls about their father leaving them, making excuses about his working away. But they were now old enough to work things out for themselves, and they quickly realised that he had in fact deserted them and their mother. They tried their hardest to help and comfort her, as they saw from the start that she was struggling to cope alone, but things got worse as the weeks passed, while the house cruelly echoed their father's absence.

They noticed then that their mother had begun drinking every day, and throughout the day, starting at breakfast and continuing well into the evening when they returned from school. In the past, both parents had enjoyed a drink together in the evenings, but it was never an issue, and it had always made them merry and fun loving with their girls. But now it was no longer just one social drink, but she would finish a whole bottle of wine during the day, and then more in the evenings as she sat alone ruminating over her situation in front of her distraught daughters.

Her constant drinking slowly took hold of her, until she was unable to stop drinking, like a total dependence against the pain she was feeling. It was one of those vicious circles many people fall victim to: the more she thought about her husband and what had happened, the more she would drink to forget about it, until it reached the stage where she couldn't stop. She would become so intoxicated at times as not to remember what she'd done, or what was happening to her, and her daughters often had to get themselves ready for school and cook their own meals, as well as keep the house in order as best they could.

During her sober moments, Veronica realised that her current situation was unsustainable, and she thought long and hard while seeking a lasting solution, for both her own and her daughters' wellbeing. She knew inside that she must forget her past relationship with her husband, painful though such an idea was. She was also unable to provide adequate care for her two daughters because of her excessive drinking, and she often felt depressed to the point of not wanting to live anymore, although the presence of her daughters kept her going.

Formerly, she had attended church regularly with her husband and children, although that had stopped about a year before. But now, in a serious moment, she decided to visit her local catholic priest in the hope of finding some friendly and understanding advice.

She contacted the parish priest, Father Damien, and asked if she could visit him privately to talk about some problems. He agreed and they made an appointment. She managed to remain sober and kept the appointment, recounting her story and telling him what was happening to her now with her drinking problem and how her daughters were being neglected because of it, and hoping he might be able to offer some advice and help.

Father Damien had been the parish priest at the Sacred Heart of Jesus church for over twenty years, and he had a vast experience of helping parishioners with their various issues. His advice was consistently sensible, and his parishioners trusted him. When Carol visited and told him her story and the trouble she was now going through, he suggested that she might place her two children temporarily into a Catholic children's home, at least until she overcame her drinking habit.

He explained that it was a loving and caring society that would look after her children while she could register herself into a rehabilitation centre and learn to control and eventually overcome her drinking habit. She confessed to him that she could no longer look after or feed the girls as she had before, sometimes providing only one meal a day, if that, and not washing their clothes as they needed them and all the other daily routines growing children need and expect. This neglect caused her even more anxiety as her daughters looked at her more and more with mixed confusion and anger in their eyes.

Carol was now thirteen years old, while Elizabeth was twelve, and both were beginning to look uncared for and undernourished, whereas they needed a lot more attention and understanding as they entered their teenage years. The priest told her again that this wasn't a good situation for them to be in. Veronica listened in silence, feeling a huge burden of guilt and shame, as she knew the girls depended upon her alone now that their father had abandoned them, and so she agreed it would be a good idea for them to go into care for a while until she could pull herself together again. Father Damien told her it was the best solution and said he would arrange with the Mother Superior to take the children into her care.

And that is the story which led to Mother Superior Colette waiting for the two children of a certain Mrs. Veronica Williams to come into her care. She had learnt from Father Damien's report that Veronica Williams had become addicted to alcohol after her husband had abandoned her and her children, and was now a chronic alcoholic, all of which affected her health and her whole life, as well as that of her two young children, who were being grossly neglected.

***

Before becoming a nun, Mother Superior Colette, still known as Rebecca Samuels back then, had sailed through her school years with ease and then went on to college, from where she graduated with high grades. She then worked in retail as a sales manager, a post in which she excelled, and was eventually promoted to an executive position.

Her parents, devout Catholics from Ireland, had settled in England before she was born, and she was an only child who had enjoyed attending church every Sunday with them. She'd received her first communion at the age of seven and was confirmed upon turning eleven. She'd always appeared to be a devoted child; devotion which increased as she grew up.

Her parents were immensely proud of her accomplishments and waited with expectant joy for her to find a suitable catholic suitor whom she would eventually marry and then present them with much-longed-for grandchildren.

But as time passed, she appeared quite indifferent to and uninterested in any of the young men that attended her church, and with whom her parents always encouraged her to communicate with. She seemed far more interested in her work, and the sermons and scriptures she heard and studied at the church. And so, when one day she expressed to them her desire to become a nun, they weren't unduly surprised, although a little disappointed all the same. But they fully understood what she believed to be her divine calling and so they gave her their full blessing.

And so it was that Rebecca Samuels entered the closeted religious life as a novice nun at the age of twenty-three, adopting the title of Sister Colette. She proved to be a conscientious novice, never missing mass or prayers, of which there were many throughout each day, from dawn to nightfall, and working at the given tasks with a happy smile and dedication that earned her the reputation of being a happy and helpful soul whom all could depend upon.

She rapidly completed her novitiate and so joined in the convent life with her whole being, which impressed all those in power above her, marking her out in the hierarchy. A few years later, when the actual Mother Superior passed away at a ripe old age, it just seemed a natural course of events for her be nominated to be the next Mother Superior, even though she didn't think herself worthy of the position at that time.

After several weeks of prayer and meditation, she duly took a solemn vow of obedience, and then the local Bishop inaugurated her as the Mother Superior of the convent, in which role she was soon held in great respect by all the other nuns in her convent, despite being a lot younger than most Mother Superiors.

She quickly became known as a kind, understanding and compassionate person, and since taking up her office she has encouraged many young women to pursue a vocation in the religious life, even though it can seem more difficult for young women to take their vows and become nuns in the present day. But she always enjoyed a new challenge, and when Father Damien spoke to her about the case of Veronica Williams, she felt at once that it was her duty to become involved and do her utmost to be of assistance.

***

Veronica had decided that she must get some help, otherwise she might lose her children permanently, something she didn't want to happen. That was when Father Damien had spoken with Mother Superior Colette, and together they had set things in motion for the children to be temporarily taken into the care of the convent.

Veronica then explained to her children that she must spend some time in a special clinic until she got back to normal, and they would be taken care of properly by some very kind people until she was fit enough to take them back home. She thought they had understood and felt relieved in herself. She knew it was for the best of them all in the long run.

Father Damien arranged to pick them up and drive them to the convent once everything had been arranged. Both children were upset to leave their mother, as they'd never been apart before, and they felt confused about leaving their home to enter such a place, but they also knew that they had to accept the new situation.

On their arrival, the Mother Superior received the two girls with a friendly greeting and smile, informing them again that their mother was going into hospital for some special treatment, and that they would stay at the children's home only temporarily, returning to their mother once she had recovered, which she hoped wouldn't be too long.

She then took them to the dining area, where they were given a tasty dinner and some orange juice, and she guessed that they hadn't had such a good meal in a long time as she watched them wolf it all down ravenously. After the meal, they were taken to the room where they would be sleeping, a small dormitory with six beds, and each bed had a cupboard for the children to use and store their personal belongings.

Carol and Elizabeth had brought with them only a few clothes and other belongings, not knowing how long they would have to stay there. The Sister in charge of the dormitory helped them unpack and arrange their affairs in their designated cupboards, and they both appeared happier then and quite resigned to living in this new and unfamiliar environment. When this was done, they were taken out to visit the home and meet the other residents.

A few children were playing outside in the playground area, where there was a lot of equipment and activities for the children's use. Other children were watching television or playing games in one of the living rooms put to their use. It all seemed to be very cozy and friendly as they were introduced to the other children, made them feel welcome from the start.

A certain Mrs. Watkins had worked at the home for ten years as a housemother and nurse, while her husband, Burt, also worked there as caretaker and handyman. She had a good rapport with the children and the nuns, being responsible for any medical or other needs. Before working at the children's home, she had been a nurse at the local General Hospital and so held an SRN qualification. When any of the children fell ill, she would nurse and look after them, making sure they received the right treatment. And if it was more serious, she would contact the local doctor's surgery, who would then visit the young patients. She did love working with the children, finding it very satisfying.

Mr. Watkins had been a local handyman before taking up his post at the convent along with his wife, and he had a great passion for gardening. Quite a few of the nuns shared this passion, and he often received help from them. He loved his job, and the children would always speak with him when he was working in the garden or at other tasks. There were a few apple trees growing there, and in the summer, he would always give the children apples to eat when they were ripe.

The home relied upon funding from the local County Council, with other funding coming from different organisations. The buildings were well kept, and the running of the home was inspected yearly by Ofsted. Some of the children attended nearby schools, while the younger ones were taught by nuns who held teaching degrees and had been teachers in their former lives.

The home was well known and firmly established in the community, which supported and took an active role in certain events for the children, and Veronica's daughters soon felt at home there, but without forgetting their mother.

Chapter 2

The first thing Veronica did once her children were safely installed at the children's home was to contact Alcoholics Anonymous and ask to attend one of their group meetings. She did this then and listened to some of the other people present at the meeting as they talked about their own problems with drinking.

She then spoke with the responsible of the group, a Mr. Dennis Thompson, telling him all about her problems and the reasons she had started drinking so heavily, while he listened attentively, having no doubt heard so many similar stories in monitoring the group. He recommended that she should talk with her doctor as a first step, and to be frank with him about her problem, impressing upon him her genuine desire to overcome the alcoholism which was destroying her life. He told her then that she could always attend their meetings in the future and get friendly advice about her drinking.

After talking with her Doctor, he recommended that she seek treatment at a rehabilitation facility. He would write a referral letter for her to get in touch with a rehabilitation clinic and so schedule an appointment.

Two weeks later she received an appointment letter from a specialised institution to see one of their doctors, and where, after assessment, she could receive help with her drinking habit. If accepted, she would have to stay at the institution for a minimum of twelve weeks while undergoing therapy to cure her of her addiction.

She arrived early at the detox centre for her 10:00am appointment, feeling quite nervous. A receptionist received her and asked a lot of personal questions while filling in a form, including her name and date of birth and family and work status, and other things concerning her health and mental health, all of which her assigned doctor would study before she met him.

Shortly after this she was called into the doctor's office, where he told her he was pleased to meet her and asked her to take a seat. His name was Doctor Gerald Smith, and he looked to be in his early forties and quite smartly dressed. She felt at ease straight away, as he had a friendly manner of speaking which he'd no doubt refined over years of working with such patients. Now, as Veronica sat before him, he began asking questions.

"When did you last have a drink?" he asked in a matter-of-fact tone, taking notes.

"Yesterday evening," she replied.

"And why would you like to be admitted here?" he went on.

"So that I can stop drinking...I want to get help for my craving and addiction to alcohol."

"But what caused you to start drinking, and why do you want to stop now?"

"Well, right now I'm facing a lot of problems, including being unemployed and looking after my children properly, as well as being in debt and dealing with anger issues caused by drinking."

"Do you see yourself as being an alcoholic?"

"Yes," she answered nervously. "I think I am."

"Well, Veronica, that is the first step to a cure, admitting that you are an alcoholic."

She didn't reply but just sat there quietly.

He then explained to her the details of the detox programme carried out in the clinic and said that they could help her to stop drinking, but only if she agreed to cooperate fully.

"I will appoint a 'friend' and monitor who will watch over and be responsible for you the whole time you will be here. Would you have you any objections to that?"

"No, that would be fine, I think. But how long would I have to be here before I can go home safely and not be tempted to drink again?"

"Well, there's no set time or limits, as each patient's case is unique and different, of course. A lot will depend upon your own strength of will and commitment to get cured, which are crucial for the detox programme's success. But we will provide you with unwavering support throughout the entire process."

"Thank you, doctor...."

"Okay, Veronica, if you go back to the waiting room the receptionist will give you a date when you can start your course of treatment here, and we'll make this soon as possible. I understand that your children have been placed into temporary care?"

"Yes...and that is the main reason I'd like to start this treatment as soon as possible..."

"Well, don't worry, I shall see to it that we find a place for you as quickly as we can..." he smiled at her.

"Oh, thank you, doctor..."

And she left the clinic in a far more positive frame of mind than she had entered a couple of hours before. Perhaps there was still hope for her after all.

Chapter 3

Shortly after this, Veronica received a letter from the National Health Service giving a date and time for her to enter the detox centre. It was in two days' time and listed what she needed to bring with her. She started to pack a bag, pleased to be she going and getting some help, although she was anxious in not knowing what to expect. She also had doubts about if she could succeed in stopping her drinking, but she knew she had to for the sake of her children.

She was in herself quite an intelligent person and had attended a Grammar School, where she'd passed her exams with good grades. She then studied at Leicester University and achieved a degree in business studies, working in management at a large corporation until the birth of her children.

She arrived at the detox centre at nine o'clock on the appointed day and was welcomed by a receptionist.

"Good morning. I'll show you to your room and let you get settled, and then I'll show you around the facility and introduce you to some of the other people who are staying here."

"Thank you..."

The room looked comfortable and was furnished with a bed, a desk and chair, and there was also a television. She felt less anxious as she unpacked her case, and thought about her children, wondering how they were coping with their own move to the care home.

She felt desperate for a drink, and her hands were shaking slightly. Her last drink had been the night before, and she'd forced herself not to drink that morning before leaving home. She sat quietly in the chair for a moment before moving to the window to gaze blanky out. She felt really unsettled then and thought she would have to leave and return home as she couldn't face not having a drink at that moment to help calm her nerves.

But there was a knock on the door when she opened it, she found a nurse standing there with a friendly smile.

"Hello, Veronica, pleased to meet you," the nurse said as she entered the room. "Have you settled in yet?"

"No, I haven't," she replied. "And I think I'll have to go back home...I don't think I'll be able to stay here like this..."

"Well, a lot of people feel the same when they first come here," the nurse told her warmly. "So don't worry too much about it. Just sit down a moment and try to relax, and I'll bring you something that will help calm you down."

She did as the nurse said, but she still felt the overpowering need for a drink, for which she was now desperate. The nurse returned a few minutes later with a full glass.

"Drink this," she told Veronica, handing her the glass. "And you'll soon feel better. If any time you'd like more, just press the buzzer over there and I'll bring you another drink. Now drink this and let me know how you find it. I'll be back in a little while to see how you feel."

Veronica sipped hesitantly at first but then finished it rapidly. She felt it did steady her nerves a little, and she wondered what it was.

When the nurse returned after thirty minutes or so, she found Veronica still sitting on her chair but looking a lot more relaxed now.

"If you feel ready now, I'll give you a tour of all our facilities and introduce you to some of the other people staying here," she told her.

Veronica agreed, and they went together around the centre, where Veronica took in what she could and nodded to any other patients she passed. The nurse also gave her the mealtimes and showed her all the facilities she could use at her will. She was already feeling a lot better in herself.

"Could I have another one of those drinks please," she then asked the nurse.

"Of course," the nurse replied. "Where would you like it? You can either sit in the sitting room or have it in your room?"

"I think I'd like it in my room, please…"

The nurse fetched the drink and then led her back to her room.

"Dinner will be served at six o'clock in the main dining area, so please come down, and I'll help you."

"Thank you. That's very kind of you."

And that was how Veronica began her treatment at the detox clinic.

Chapter 4

Veronica's two daughters we're settling in quite well at the children's home, joining in the communal life and slowly making new friends with some of the other children. The nuns were pleased with the way they had adapted and made no waves at all, as newcomers could sometimes be disruptive and difficult to handle.

But then some of the nuns became a little concerned about Carol, the older sister, as they noticed differences in her from her younger sister, Elizabeth. She began to complain of an upset stomach after eating some of the meals, and so they decided to take her to the local surgery for a thorough check-up.

The doctor duly examined her but could find nothing obviously wrong, and so he suggested that she visit the hospital for some in-depth scans and analyses to discover what, if anything, was wrong with her.

They received an appointment letter a few days later, and Mrs. Watkins accompanied her to the hospital. She underwent several different scans and tests over a few hours, some of which were quite intrusive and upsetting, although she remained calm and stoic through it all. But on returning to the home, she went straight to bed and slept through the rest of the day, quite exhausted. It had become a worry then for all the staff, who realised that something was perhaps seriously wrong with her.

Shortly after, she was called to attend the hospital again, where the doctor informed Mrs. Watson of the results of the tests Carol had undergone. She was suffering from both Crohn's disease and celiacs disease. These were both illnesses that affected the digestive system, which explained why Carol had been experiencing difficulties with food and her diet.

Both diseases could be treated by observing a strict diet, mostly gluten free, and some medication was available for treating Crohn's Disease. The doctor told them that he would make an appointment for Carol to see a nutritionist at the hospital. Carol seemed quite disinterested in all this, remaining silent and aloof.

On the way home, they stopped at a local cafe for some refreshments. Carol again remained silent, not say anything about the hospital visit to Mrs. Watkins but just staring blankly out of the window. Mrs. Watkins was surprised at this reaction and tried to explain to Carol the dietary treatment she would have to follow from now on, but Carol remained uninterested.

A week later they received a letter from the hospital inviting Carol to see the nutritionist, who explained to them both the importance of adhering to the diet which had been composed for Carol to follow, and to take the medication that had been prescribed. She should then very soon be back to normal. Again, Carol absorbed all this in a blank silence.

Mrs. Watkins had become increasingly concerned about the girl's behaviour, as she appeared constantly anxious and suffered violent mood swings, keeping herself to herself and barely mixing with the other children at all. She believed this could be linked to her situation and the fact that she was missing her mother, and now her diagnosis was another problem she must learn to live with.

Mrs. Watkins decided then to keep notes about her behaviour, so that if the need arose, she could return to the doctor and talk with him about the girl's problems. She was, of course, also at that stage of her development wherein her mind and body were both transforming from childhood to adolescence, which is often a difficult time for any child, and more so when the mother is absent, as Mrs. Watkins knew well from long experience.

Carol's younger sister Elizabeth was in complete contrast to her, mixing well with the other children and helping wherever she could. She really enjoyed working in the kitchens with small tasks and doing the washing-up. She was turning into a very friendly and likeable young girl, and the nuns and staff found her to be a comforting and understanding presence for her older sister.

She never openly hinted that she was missing her mother and was quite happy to sit in the chapel with the nuns during their daily prayer sessions, and she always attended mass on Sunday mornings. She once confessed to Sister Juliana that she loved Jesus and would like to become a nun when she was older. But Sister Juliana told her that she was still too young to think about such things and advised her to wait until she was older to reevaluate her feelings on the subject.

On one occasion some of the nuns found Elizabeth alone in the chapel, on her knees and praying devoutly. They expressed surprise at her keen interest in the church and convent life and were concerned that her mother might not appreciate the religious influence from the home at such an early age. But Elizabeth remained oblivious of any such feelings. She was still a child adapting to her special circumstances and enjoying the calm of the chapel.

Carol was totally the opposite about that side of the home's social life, and she didn't attend chapel or take part in the weekly mass. The nuns never obliged any of the children to take part in their services, as it was the policy of the home not to force the children to follow any religion. One of the conditions of the Social Services that ran the home was that the children had to be cared for independently from the Catholic Church and its teachings.

One of the young boys at the home, Joseph Fowler, had been there now for nine years. He had been placed there at the age of four, after both his parents had been tragically killed in a car accident. He had no other relatives and had been placed temporarily with foster parents, before being taken in by the children's home. He'd remained there then, as they never found any family willing to adopt him.

He'd grown up to be mostly independent and was quite a handful for the nuns to cope with at times. But he'd always been helpful regarding the other children, becoming a kind of figurehead for any newcomers to confide in. He didn't really care much for the church's teachings, and so he never paid attention when attending the Sunday mass. His parents had been devout Catholics, but again he was never forced to take part in the services.

He was an outgoing boy, very popular with the other children, and when Carol and Elizabeth arrived, he was quick to befriend them, particularly Carol, who was roughly the same age. They began to spend a lot of time together then and could often be found sitting and talking together in the garden.

Mother Superior Colette soon noticed that they had become close and thought this was a good thing for them both, as most of the other children were a lot younger. It was also a good sign, as Carol had been spending far too much time alone, and Mother Superior Colette knew that Joseph was a good companion for her. She sometimes met them and asked how they were getting along, and they were always friendly and polite. But sometimes it was difficult for the nuns to make conversation with them, as if they were exiting in their own private world.

Chapter 5

Veronica had adapted well to life at the Detox Centre, while following the programme set up for her. She was feeling much better and joined in some of the activities. She attended yoga lessons three times a week and took part in the exercises with other residents. She also took medication for her depression caused by drinking. She would have a private session with a counsellor twice a week to discuss her alcohol addiction. It was explained to her that alcohol dependency is akin to drug addiction, in that it is an addiction they cannot control.

Counselling was very good for her, and it gave her a different perspective on her life. She would often ask about her two daughters and was given updates on their situation. She wasn't told about Carol's medical problems as they were concerned this might trigger a relapse, and so they decided it better for her not to know her daughter's condition at that time. It wasn't considered to be a serious condition.

She had been in the Detox Centre for four weeks when the doctor explained that she would have to stay for another three months, to show that she could finally do without drinking any alcohol. He asked her how she was getting on, and how she felt in herself now.

"I'm getting along fine now that I've settled in here, and I feel so much better in myself," she replied.

"Well, that's good to hear. And you may stop your medication if you feel confident enough to resist the temptation of drinking again".

"Thank you, doctor. That would be good, because the medication does make me feel tired."

"Are you still feeling down and depressed sometimes?"

"Only now and again, when I have a bad day. But I feel quite happy most of the time now, and I'm glad to have stopped drinking, because I think if I hadn't, I might have drunk myself into the grave…"

"Well, I'm glad that's no longer the case," the doctor chuckled. "And how are you getting on with your personal carer?"

"All right, I think. He's been very supportive, and he's very good to talk with sometimes when I need advice about things."

"That's good. Now I would like to do some blood tests if you are okay with that?"

"Yes, of course…"

She left the doctor feeling quite happy again and began thinking about her future life after leaving the Detox Centre. She had aspired to work in book publishing before this crisis, and she hoped this might happen, but she knew that first she must remain strong and committed to overcoming her drinking problem. She looked at photos of her daughters and sighed heavily. They were possibly the biggest incentive she had now through all her treatment.

Chapter 6

At the children's home, Carol was acting rather bizarrely at times and was causing some concern for the staff. Sister Colette was keeping a closer watch on her and eventually decided to accompany her to the local health clinic for an assessment of her mental health and general wellbeing. She had noticed that Carol could often be seen sitting alone and staring blankly into space and often talking to herself, as if oblivious of everything around her. She booked an appointment at the clinic and went along with Mrs. Watkins and Carol to see the doctor.

Sister Colette went in alone to see the doctor to explain her worries and the situation with Carol, while Mrs. Watkins waited outside with Carol. The doctor then asked for Carol to come into the surgery so he could talk with her and try to discover what might be troubling her, then assess if she needed some kind of specialist help.

He decided to refer her for a mental health examination with a psychiatrist at the local hospital and told Sister Colette that they would hear from the hospital shortly.

A couple of weeks later they attended an appointment with Professor William Jolly, a child psychiatrist. He wanted to talk to Carol along with Mrs Watkins, who asked her if she was comfortable with meeting this man. She said that she was. He came out and asked them both to come into his office.

He introduced himself to Carol and told her to call him William rather than doctor. She didn't answer but just sat there looking blankly at him.

"How are you today, Carol?" he asked.

"I'm ok," she answered in a quiet voice.

"Can you tell me a little bit about yourself, then?"

"I'm thirteen years old, and I live with Mrs. Watkins in the children's home. "And I would like to see my mum…"

"Yes, of course, that's quite understandable. But you do know that she's been ill and must undergo treatment for a few weeks, don't you?"

"Yes, of course…"

"But let's talk about you, shall we. I understand that you've been talking to yourself quite a lot lately, so can you tell me something about that?"

Carol looked sternly at Mrs. Watkins for a moment, knowing at once that she must have spoken to the doctor about this. She felt it as a betrayal of confidence but let it go. She simply wanted for the interview to be over and then go back to her solitary musings at the home.

"Well, yes, I do have like a friend who I can talk to…and she tells me what to do sometimes, you see…"

"I see, yes. But what do you mean by a friend?" the doctor asked, glad that he had got her talking.

"She's just a friend who comes and talks to me when I feel a bit sad..."

"And what does she say to you?"

"She just tells me to do things."

"I see. And does she talk to you often?"

"Yes, every day usually..."

"Does she have a name?"

"Yes, her name's Betty..."

"And what sort of things does she tell you to do?"

"Well, we just talk like girls mostly, but sometimes she tells me to do naughty things..."

"And do you do the naughty things?"

"Sometimes, yes..."

"Can you tell me what sort of things you do?"

"She tells me to drop my cup on the floor to spill it, and not to eat my dinner in case someone is trying to poison me..."

"I see. But do you usually eat all your dinner?"

"Not if she tells me not to."

"Okay, I see...I have just one more question for you today, Carol. Do you always do everything she tells you to do?"

"Yes, I do..."

He scribbled some notes and then spoke with Mrs. Watkins, asking a few questions about Carol's health and behaviour at the home. Carol felt as if they were discussing someone else, as if she were absent in herself now the doctor had asked his questions.

"Well, that's all for today, I think," he told them then with a smile. "But I would like to see you again next week if that's okay?"

"Yes, all right," Carol replied.

With that he shook them both by the hand and they left his office.

***

The following week they attended the next appointment, during which the psychiatrist chatted again with Carol, asking questions and trying to prise answers that would give him more insight into the girl's character and psyche. He asked about her mood swings, and as she didn't seem to understand what that meant, he asked if she might feel fed up on certain days and on other days happy?

Carol told him that on some days she really did feel fed up and very bored, especially if she was doing boring things, like helping with chores around the home and sometimes at school and her schoolwork, where she often had difficulty paying attention. Her best moments were usually when she was able to be alone, or else with her close friend at the home, Joseph.

The doctor then spoke with Mrs. Watkins, telling her he would have a report ready in a week or so, and he would let them know his diagnosis then. They left the clinic then and returned to the home, where Joseph Fowler was waiting near the entrance for Carol.

"Hello Carol, are you all, right?" he asked.

"Yes, I'm fine Joe," she told him, and they went off together into the garden.

Mrs. Watkins watched them go with a worried frown on her face.

***

They duly returned to the hospital to meet with the psychiatrist again and to hear his diagnosis. Mrs. Watkins helped Carol to get ready early, but the girl wasn't really interested and didn't seem to care what might happen to her.

"Do you think they'll keep me in the hospital?" she asked then in a worried tone.

"Of course they won't," Mrs. Watkins told her. "It's just to find out what's been troubling you lately, that's all. We'll be back here in no time, so don't worry about that…"

"Well, that's okay then," Carol sighed, and she seemed reassured and more at ease then.

At the hospital they were shown into the psychiatrist's office again, and he greeted them warmly with a smile.

"Good morning. How are you, Carol?"

"I'm ok, thanks," Carol answered quietly, avoiding his direct gaze.

"Well now, after talking with you at our last meetings, and after consulting some of my colleagues, I think we can safely say that you have a condition commonly known as ADHD. This makes it difficult for you to pay attention and concentrate sometimes, especially at school and other places where you might be expected to do something that you object to internally."

"Oh, dear," Mrs. Watkins said. "That does sound rather serious..."

Carol didn't seem to take any notice of what the doctor said but just sat there vaguely listening.

"Well, it isn't such a serious problem," the doctor went on. "I can prescribe some medication that will help Carol feel a lot better in her everyday life, and we will monitor her of course on a regular basis to check on her progress."

"Thank you, doctor. That will be a help, I'm sure."

"Of course. So, Carol, try not to worry too much about things, and I'm sure we'll be able to help you overcome your problems and let you live a normal life again. I would like to see you again in four weeks' time to see how you're getting on with the medication, and then we'll take it from there. Okay?"

"Yes, okay..." Carol answered softly, with almost a smile.

With that they left the office and took the doctor's prescription to the pharmacy in the hospital to pick up the medication. Then they returned to the home, with Carol seeming a lot less troubled than on going to the hospital. On arrival, Joeseph was again waiting at the entrance. Carol ran straight to him and sat beside him. Mrs. Watkins sighed and returned to her duties.

Chapter 7

After eleven weeks in the Rehab Centre, Veronica had been extraordinarily successful in overcoming and controlling her dependence upon alcohol, and she was ready for an assessment to ascertain if she was well enough to return home. She was duly called for an interview with Doctor Smith.

"Good morning, Veronica. How are you today?"

"I'm very well, thank you, Doctor. And I can hardly wait to see my children and have them back at home with me."

"Well, that's a positive attitude," the Doctor told her. "But I still need to ask you a few questions to assess if you are well enough to be discharged from the centre."

"Yes, of course, I understand."

"Well, first off, do you ever feel the urge or need to have a drink now? I mean, if you're feeling a bit off-colour or depressed on certain days?"

"No, not now. I really do feel all that's been put behind me and I really do want to get back to my life as it was, working and looking after my daughters."

"That is good to hear, and you should congratulate yourself on your progress here. But do you think you could manage on your own now, without our constant help and care?"

"Yes, doctor, I'm sure I can. I've been thinking a lot about what I am going to do in the future now that my head is clear again and free from my drink problem."

"Good, that does reassure me. So, I think I can authorise your discharge now, but I would recommend that you remain on your own at home for a little while and leave your children where they are for now, just to see how you get along in the outside world again."

"Yes, I understand," she told the doctor, hiding her impatience and slight disappointment as best she could.

"You will be able to contact your monitor here at any time if you feel you need some help or support, and so you mustn't hesitate to do so whenever you want to. We will continue our own monitoring as well, of course, but I feel quite sure that you have come through the worst and will quickly pick up your normal life again. Just remember that we are all here if you need us."

"Thank you, doctor. That will be good to know…"

"Now I'll get a nurse to give you a routine checkup before you leave and we'll send the results to your own doctor, if that's okay with you?"

"Yes, of course…"

"All right then. When you are packed and ready to leave, the receptionist will ask you to sign a discharge form, and then you'll be free to go home."

"Thank you, doctor. You've all been extremely helpful to me, and I really appreciate what you've done for me. I feel sure that I'll be okay again from now on."

"Well, that's what we're here for, and we do enjoy having success stories, believe me. I wish you all the best for the future. Goodbye."

"Goodbye, Doctor…"

Veronica returned to her room and quickly packed her belongings, ready to leave the centre as quickly as she could. A nurse came and carried out the routine tests the doctor had mentioned, and then at the reception she signed her discharge form. All that remained was for her to call a taxi and leave the centre for the last time, as she hoped.

She felt very pleased with herself, having achieved all she had come there to achieve, and she was impatient to get home and start thinking and planning for the future. Getting her children back was, of course, the most pressing thing on her mind. She planned to go and visit them and find out how they'd been coping with the separation. But she felt she must follow the doctor's advice and wait some time before actually bringing them back home to live with her again. Better be prudent and sure rather than rush into anything and be sorry. She felt sure she had learnt her lesson once and for all.

Chapter 8

The day after leaving the Rehab Centre, Veronica called the home and spoke with the Mother Superior, asking if it would be okay for her to visit her children. She was told that she'd be more than welcome, and the girls would be delighted to see her again after so long a separation. It would be preferable for her to come in the afternoon, when the children would have more free time to talk with her.

She was highly excited at the prospect of being with her daughters again but wondered what sort of reception she might receive. It had been a three-month separation, and she knew from experience how that can seem a very long period in a child's life and development. She hoped they would still understand how necessary it had been at the time.

She found them waiting for her in the garden when she arrived, as they'd been told she was coming. They ran towards her and hugged and kissed her warmly, and they all had tears in their eyes. Veronica was overwhelmed by such a warm greeting, and her fears of being rejected fell away to nothing. She held their hands and stared warmly into their eyes, remembering that they were her children and that they mattered more than anything else in her life. She saw that they still loved her and regarded her as their mother, and that's what mattered most for all of them right then.

Once calmed down, they began to chat with their mother about all they had been through since being at the home without her. She learned then about Carol's ill-health and the hospital visits, which struck her as cruel, as she hadn't been informed at the Rehab Clinic, for reasons she well knew. But Carol reassured her, she was all right now and taking medication to help her and keep her normal.

As for Elizabeth, she spoke mostly about the nuns she had befriended and the chapel services she attended every day, morning and evening, and how much she would like to become a nun herself when she was old enough. Veronica smiled and hugged her again, believing it to be just a childish fad she would grow out of as she got older.

Then Carol asked her if she had giving up drinking now, and she understood why.

"Yes, I have," she told her. "It was a dark period, I know, and so unfair on you both. But now I have completely overcome it and won't ever go back to that way of life again, I promise you both."

"Does that mean we can come home with you now, then?" Carol asked.

"Well, not today, no…the doctor wants me to stay on my own a little while to be sure I can cope again, so you'll need to be patient a little while longer, I'm afraid…but very soon I'll come to collect you, I promise."

"How long will that be?" Carol asked, disappointment written across her face.

"Not long, really…I just need to show them that you'll be fine with me again, then everything will be just as it was before all this happened."

"Well, I don't mind staying here, actually," Elizabeth then stated with a smile.

"Oh, why not?" Veronica asked.

"She's turned into a real little Jesus baby…" Carol told her with a smirk.

"Oh no I haven't!" Elizabeth snorted. "Just because you don't believe any of it…"

"Well, let's not argue now," Veronica told them, holding their hands again. "We'll soon be all together again and take up where we left off."

"But the nuns have told me I can stay here with them and study and pray to become a nun one day if you agree to that, so I'm not being awkward, really," Elizabeth told her. "I really do want to be a nun one day, you see…"

Veronica was surprised at this attitude, as she'd never been particularly religious before, and she wondered how much influence this place and the nuns were exerting over the children they had to care for. But she pushed that aside for the moment, still happy to be with them and to be able to talk and hold their hands as before, as every mother should.

"Well, my little darling, we'll see how things go later when you're back home with me and go to school and we're like a family again with everything as before. All right?"

"Oh, all right…but will daddy be back as well?" she asked, casting a dark shadow over the joy of their reunion.

"No," Veronica told them clearly. "He won't be coming back, I'm afraid, but you will be able to see him whenever you want to. He is still your father., and he still loves you and cares about you, no matter what else happens."

The two girls looked at each other and frowned. They had understood, she knew.

A couple of hours later Veronica decided to leave. She also needed to assess all that had happened and all she had heard from her daughters. She was confident that when they did return home, she would be able to cope and look after them as they needed and deserved.

They clung hard to her as she said her goodbyes, with more tears and kisses, and it was hard for her to leave them again. But she told herself she must stay strong and be there whenever they needed her. That's what mothers did, no matter what.

Back home that evening, alone, with tears streaming down her face, she realised just how much she had missed her two children and how much they really meant to her. Reflecting on the bad impact alcohol had inflicted upon her and her loved ones, she vowed then to turn her life around and to recreate a stable home for them all.

Chapter 9

A few days after her visit, Veronica received a letter that hit her like a bombshell:

Dear Veronica

I am sorry to have to inform you that your husband, Michael, has suddenly passed away. He suffered a devastating ruptured aneurysm and collapsed at home, and I immediately called the emergency paramedics. But when they arrived and examined him, they told me there was nothing they could do. He was dead when they got there, and there was nothing I could have done to help him.

I am sorry to have to tell you this, and I know that you don't wish to speak with me because of what happened between us, but I know that Michael kept in touch with you to ask how his children were getting on. So could you please inform Carol and Elizabeth about their father's death. I know he thought the world of them.

I will keep you updated when the funeral arrangements have been made.

Yours sincerely,

Margaret.

Veronica was in total shock after reading this over again. She also wondered how an apparently healthy young man could succumb to such an unexpected attack. She shed a few tears, knowing that she still harboured deep feelings of love for him and still perplexed about why he had suddenly left her and the children when he did. She worried then about how she was going to tell the children that their father had died. She knew that she would have to.

She felt her mind in turmoil and asked herself what else could possibly go wrong in her life. She also knew that there was a bottle of wine stashed away in a cupboard in the kitchen, and the temptation crept in again for her to have a drink and so forget all the problems. But she knew that she mustn't. The children would need her more than ever now, and they were her main priority.

She called to her monitor at the Rehab Centre and told him about her situation. He said he would come round to see her as soon as he could get away, and an hour later he was there with her. He saw at once how upset she was, and so he made her some coffee and they sat together to talk over her situation, and that of her children, whom she had to inform about their father's unexpected death.

He felt at once what a terrible situation Veronica found herself in, and he offered to go with her to visit the children at the convent home to tell them about the loss of their father. He also suggested that she call the Mother Superior and share with her the tragic news before going to see the children.

He stayed with her for a couple of hours, wanting to be certain that she wouldn't slide back into her drinking habit on account of this huge upset. He was reassured when, after a little while, she opened a cupboard and took out a bottle of wine, which she opened in front of him and then poured it down the sink.

"You see," she told him, sure in her own mind that she would never drink again. "You don't have to worry about me in that way ever again..."

He hugged her, reassured now that she would be okay. He told her to contact him if ever she needed someone to talk with again, and shortly afterwards he left her alone.

She called the Mother Superior at the home then to let her know what had happened, and to schedule another visit to tell her children the dreadful news and try her best to comfort them. She was told to come the following day.

At the children's home, the Mother Superior greeted her and invited her into her office, where she shared details about her husband and what had happened to him so unexpectedly. Sister Colette listened with a grave regard and then agreed with her that she must tell her daughters, as they had a right to know, and they were at an age now to understand and accept. She would call them into the office and then leave her alone with them for a while, but she also said that the whole staff would be informed and would be on hand to help support the two girls in their grief.

Carol and Elizabeth entered the office with slightly puzzled expressions, not knowing why their mother had come again so quickly to see them. Sister Colette ushered them in and then left them alone. The grim atmosphere let them know that something bad had happened, although they had no inkling of how serious a matter it was.

"My darlings," Veronica began in a quiet and trembling voice. "I have some terrible news to tell you..."

The two girls looked at each other and frowned, obviously thinking similar thoughts about their mother.

"You haven't started drinking again, have you?" Carol asked with a severe look of reproach.

"No, of course not!" Veronica replied firmly. "I told you before, that's all over now forever…"

"What's happened then?" Elizabeth asked, looking uneasy now.

"Well, it's not easy for me to tell you this, but it's about your father…"

"Oh? Is he coming back?" Carol asked.

"No, sadly not…you see, he had a nasty brain seizure a few days ago, and I must tell you that he passed away…"

The two girls looked at her in shock, unable to comprehend at first what she was telling them. They looked briefly at each other, still struggling to understand and process what this meant, and then they both broke down simultaneously as the wave of information swept clearly through them at last.

"You mean…he's dead?" Carol asked, her gaze more piercing than any arrow.

"Yes, dear, I'm afraid he is…"

Elizabeth let out a strident cry then that broke the air of solemnity, letting in the wind of tragedy that always bears such awful tidings. They both rushed over to their mother and fell into her arms, where they hugged and sobbed and released the raw pain of tragic news that had now invaded their whole beings. Even children must give vent to such terrible tides of grief, as though it is a part of their growing up, and none is worse or more enduring than the very first time it happens in a young life.

For a long time, they remained like that, hugging close as a reunited group of lost souls, the children sobbing and causing their mother the pain of helplessness she was feeling, wanting more than anything to take their pain unto herself and allow them to continue being carefree in their already slightly broken childhood. She herself suffered again a huge feeling of guilt, knowing that she was to blame, at least in part, for the uprooting they had already lived through. Now she must find a huge inner strength to be able to remedy all the wrongs that had assailed them without warning.

The Mother Superior returned after a while and comforted the girls, telling them that they must be strong, for their mother's sake, and very soon they would be able to return to their home and carry on with their lives as before. Their father would have wanted this for them. Elizabeth listened as she told them that it was God's will that such terrible things happened, even to children, but that it was all part of life, and so they should pray for their father's soul and help comfort their mother, who was grieving as much as they were. For the time being, all the sisters would be there to help them and to pray for a lasting solution, which would very soon be available. Carol listened in silence, turning her thoughts in on herself and aching to be left alone to digest these new developments.

Veronica left soon after that, heavy-hearted but glad in some respects that the sisters at the home would be there to comfort her daughters through the following days. She told them she would visit any time they needed her to, and she would let them know about future funeral arrangements, and when they might leave the home and come back to live with her. She knew that was the only viable and lasting cure they both needed. She felt them clinging to her as she left, and it felt as though they were tugging at her very heart strings. This had brought them back closer, which in other circumstances might have been seen as a blessing.

Chapter 10

Shortly after this, Veronica received a letter from her husband's partner detailing the funeral arrangements. It would be a simple funeral service to be held at Saint Marks Catholic Church. She asked Veronica to inform the children, if they wished to attend.

She thought about this with sadness, although she knew she must remain strong for the children's sake. And it was their right to attend their father's funeral if they so wished. He had abandoned them abruptly, she knew, as he had herself, but he was still their father, and even his death couldn't erase that truth. She was certain they would choose to attend.

So, she called the children's home and explained the situation to the Mother Superior, informing her of the time and date the funeral would take place, and that she thought it important for the children to attend, if they wished to. Sister Colette agreed with her and told her that she would speak to Carol and Elizabeth about it and let her know their wishes as soon as she knew. They would be ready for her to pick up on the day if they wanted to go. She felt quite sure they would.

"Would you like one of our sisters to accompany them?" she asked then.

"No, I don't think that will be necessary," Veronica replied, feeling an inner need to assert herself once and for all as their mother. "We'll be fine, I'm sure."

On the day of the funeral, Veronica collected the girls and was inwardly pleased to see how well they were looking, despite all the trauma and disruption they had been through over the past few months. Carol did appear a little upset, a lot more than did Elizabeth, but she knew that her younger daughter had always been more reflective and secretive than her older sister, and she did tend to keep her feelings to herself.

There weren't a lot of attendees at the church, a few distant relatives of Jason, her husband, and some of the partner's family, causing the atmosphere to feel intense though not openly hostile. Two sides of a coin that had been tossed and shared. There was a short requiem mass at the church, and a brief eulogy, and this was followed by a formal burial in the local cemetery. Elizabeth and Carol were both visibly distressed during the service, with Carol holding her mother's hand tightly and unable to stem her tears. Elizabeth remained calm and stoic, and her mother thought again about whether her younger daughter was really in the throes of a religious calling, young as she still was.

There was to be an intimate wake after the funeral at the partner's home, and although Veronica and the children were told that they would be welcome to attend, she knew it wouldn't be a wise thing to do, either for her or the children. When they left the cemetery they went to their own home, the first time the girls had been there since the beginning of the events that had led to this day. Veronica was feeling abandoned and lonely but determined to be strong, for her daughters' sake if nothing else. They seemed excited and delighted to be visiting their home again, even though their mother had made it plain that they would have to return to the children's home a little later.

She made them a snack-lunch, which they ate together, and then the girls went to their rooms while Veronica took a short nap. She could hear her daughters rummaging and exploring, imagining what they must be going through in their still-developing souls. They had lost their home, and their mother temporarily, and now their father was gone permanently, and that was such a lot for anyone to take in and adapt to, and even more so at such a tender age. Veronica fell into a troubled sleep then, before awaking sharply and calling the girls to order.

"We have to go now," she told them, sadly. "You have to be back for tea-time."

The girls looked at each other and then at her, pleadingly. She understood.

"Can't we just stay here with you now?" Carol asked, her voice like a stab wound in her mother's heart.

"Please…" Elizabeth added.

"Oh, my darlings, you know you can't, not for the time being, anyway. I have to show them that I can take care of you properly again and that I can get a job and work normally and all that. So, please, be patient, just a little while longer. And I promise, in a little while I will come to fetch you home forever, so don't fret about it anymore. Okay?"

"Oh, all right…" Carol replied, grumpy but understanding. She knew what her mother had been through during their separation.

She accompanied them back to the home, where they separated with a warm hug and kisses.

"We'll be together again very soon, I promise..." she repeated, before turning away quickly so they didn't see the tears rolling down her cheeks.

Chapter 11

During this period, Veronica had been thinking very hard about her own life again, and what she would like to do to earn a living and get back on her feet once and for all as an independent mother. She had always had a penchant for writing and writers and began toying with the idea of becoming an editor and agent for beginners looking to publish their first tentative works. She felt confident enough in her own literary tastes and grammatical talent to be able to offer advice and help in return for a fee, which she hoped would be a first step on the way to founding her own agency.

With this idea in mind, she began advertising her services on suitable sites across the internet and was soon receiving many e-mails asking for more details, and raising questions about the services she could offer, including proof-reading, ghost-writing, and book design and cover creation. This was encouraging, and she was determined then to go down that route and establish her own independent agency for budding – and perhaps later more established – authors. She was confident that this would allow her to earn a reasonable income while being able to work from home and take care of her daughters, which was still her main concern at that moment.

She agreed to take on a project from a woman who had written a first book, a romantic novel, as she described it, which needed proof-reading and putting into shape, correcting spelling errors and phrasing and generally making it readable for the targeted audience. She read it through, and even though she found it rather tangled in shape and narrative fluency, she felt that it was worth publishing and so produced a first contract to polish and publish the book as best she could. Every new venture must have a first step, and she felt confident that this was hers, and that it would lead to a lot more if successful.

She worked nonstop at it, from early morning until late at night and she had it completed in a couple of weeks. Exhausted, she sent the finished manuscript to various literary agents and publishers and sat waiting for news.

Amazingly, one agent replied after a week and was prepared to take it on, and so Veronica let the author know and at the same sent an invoice to be paid for her own work. It had all gone far more smoothly and quickly than she had anticipated, and that encouraged her to continue, as she'd already received dozens of enquiry letters from her own advertising campaign. This had truly restored her self-confidence, and she was convinced this was the right step to take now. She no longer thought about drinking, as most of her thoughts were focused on building up her new business venture and to bringing her daughters home.

She took on another rewriting job and received a small deposit, which boosted her confidence a little more. She began to clean and tidy up her daughter's rooms, feeling she was ready for them to come home now. She bought some new clothes and other small gifts for each of them, and could hardly wait for the day she could watch them enter their rooms and feel safe and at home with her at last, so putting the past few months of separation behind them.

She called to speak with the Mother Superior, telling her she was ready to bring the children home now, and Sister Colette was very pleased to hear how confident she sounded. She would speak to Social Services, who would have to be informed, and they would no doubt visit Veronica at home for an inspection and to judge for themselves how she was getting on. Veronica told her she understood and would wait for all this to be processed. She thought it better not to tell the girls until it had all been cleared. It should only take a few days. Her excitement grew then.

A couple of days later, a social worker came to visit Veronica at home, asking a lot of questions and inspecting the house and the girls' bedrooms, which were now immaculate and ready for them. Veronica told her about her new business venture, which was going well, and that also ticked a positive box in the social worker's documents. After a cup of tea and a friendly chat, she told Veronica she could see no obstacles for the children to be returned to her care at home. Veronica could have hugged and kissed her, but she restrained herself, thanking her for all her help.

The following day she went to meet the Mother Superior at the home, ready and excited to collect her daughters at last. Sister Colette told her she'd received confirmation from Social Services, and the girls had been told and had prepared their affairs ready to leave with her. Veronica was still excited with the speed at which all this had happened, but she controlled her emotions as best she could.

"I've got their bedrooms ready for them," she said with a smile. "And I'm really pleased about the girls coming back home to live with me. It's been a long journey for all of us, but we've come through it and I'm ready and capable of looking after my two children again…"

"I'm so happy to hear that," Sister Colette told her with a smile. "I know what you have been through, and the girls, and they are thrilled to be going home, I can assure you."

"That's good. I would like to thank you for all you have done for them, and I know they did enjoy being here with you."

"We do what we can, always. And as you know, Elizabeth really would like to stay here and join our community, although I have explained to her that this will have to wait until she is older, if she still feels the same."

"Yes, she spoke with me about this as well. We shall have to see, as they say…"

"Of course…now then, shall we go and fetch them?"

"Oh, yes…"

And later that day they were all at home again, excited and happy as families are after long separations and tragedy. Veronica watched them as they inspected their rooms and looked at the gifts and new clothes she had bought, and her heart was overflowing with love, with just a little remorse. How could she have sacrificed so much and put them through such hardships, without considering their feelings and emotions at the time? But now she had learnt the lesson, and she vowed there and then never to put them through such emotional pain and stress ever again.

That evening, curled up together on the sofa watching TV and eating a few snacks, all three felt as though they had come back from a long voyage, and it felt so good to be there together again as a family. The absence of the father still hung over them like a shadow, but the joy of being together overrode any sadness that night. They were home, and together again, and that was what counted most.

Chapter 12

Things were very quickly back to normal, or almost, with both girls attending school while their mother kept the house and looked after all their needs while also working at her new business, writing and editing and seeking contracts for the many budding writers she was now in touch with. The disruption of the past few months seemed far away now, as if in another lifetime.

Then one morning a letter arrived, looking very official with a printed address that included all three of their names. Veronica felt a little fear as she studied it, hoping it was nothing that might upset the new balance they had achieved. She opened it once the girls had left for school and read the contents slowly.

Dear Mrs. Veronica Williams and family,

I hope this letter finds you all well. I have been given your address by the partner of your late husband and father, Jason Williams.

We are the solicitors dealing with his estate and would like to inform you that you are named as beneficiaries in his last will and testament.

For this reason, we would ask you to contact our office at your earliest convenience to fix an appointment with Mr. Richard Samuels, who is the solicitor dealing with this matter.

Yours sincerely,

Mr Simon Burt, Solicitor.

Veronica called to make an appointment, and they went together to find out what it was all about. They were ushered into his office, where he opened a folder and read out what were the last wishes of Jason, husband and father in the now bereft family.

"You have been left some property," he informed them. "There are two houses in this country, and an apartment in Spain. The two houses are bequeathed one each to you, his daughters, while the apartment is for both of you. He also left the sum of £10,000 to you, Mrs. Wilson, his legal wife. Any other property and estate has been bequeathed to his partner, with whom he was living at the time of his death."

They all looked at each other with a somewhat puzzled and confused air on hearing this. Veronica knew that he had an apartment in Spain, but the two houses were a complete surprise. The solicitor interrupted their thoughts.

"The two houses and the apartment will be held in trust until both Carol and Elizabeth reach their majority, when they will then be free to do as they wish with them. I hope that is clear?"

"Yes, I think so," Veronica muttered, still a little in shock.

"Good," the solicitor said. "Well, have you any questions at all about all this? I understand it might be something of a surprise."

"It certainly is," Veronica told him with a half-smile. "Will the money be released right away?"

"Yes, of course, once the documents are drawn up and duly signed…"

"But...do we have to accept the houses?" Elizabeth then asked with a timid voice. "I mean, what if I didn't want them when I am old enough...?"

"Well, that would be entirely up to you, my dear," the solicitor chuckled. "But when you are older, I'm sure you will think differently about it all, so I shouldn't worry about it now if I were you..."

"I'm going to be a nun, you see," she told him then firmly. "And so I will have to renounce all earthly belongings..."

"I see," the solicitor said, surprised. "Well, we shall deal with all that when the time comes, don't you worry about that, my dear. And you may change your mind as you grow up...children often do, you know."

"I won't!" Elizabeth snapped with a determined stare.

"Well, let's not worry about that now," Veronica told her. "We have a lot of time to work all that out later..."

"Yes," the solicitor added. "Thank you for coming, and I hope this will help you all in what has been a difficult time. I would ask you to sign these documents now and then leave everything to me. You can contact me at any time if you need any advice, and I hope you will be able to profit from all this in the future."

They signed several official-looking documents, and then they left the office, still confused but excited as well. It had been all so unexpected. They went to a café to have some refreshment and to discuss all that had just happened.

"Well, what do you think of all that?" Veronica asked the girls.

"It's quite amazing," Carol said. "I didn't know dad had all that stuff, did you?"

"No, not really. I knew he had the apartment in Spain, but I didn't know about the houses here. It will be a good thing for both of you when you're older, that's for sure."

"But I don't want it," Elizabeth said then. "You know what I want when I'm older, don't you?"

"Of course, dear," Veronica answered. "So don't get upset about all this now. We have a lot of time to think and digest it all, and whatever you decide I will stay by you, as I've already told you. Okay?"

"Okay…you could have my house then, or Carol…or I could donate it to the convent even, couldn't I?"

"Yes, whatever you decide later. It's yours to do with as you please…"

That seemed to reassure her, and they talked about how good their lives were becoming again since they were back at home together and the future suddenly looked a lot brighter.

Veronica's business was rapidly expanding, and the money she had inherited would certainly help in making it even bigger and better. Of course, they all missed Jason terribly, and nothing could make sense of that sudden loss. But they understood now that he had been thinking of them, and that also changed their opinions about him. Life had to go on, and that day they were all determined to get on with their lives as best they could.

Chapter 13

Veronica and her daughters soon fell back into a normal routine, with Veronica running her business from home while the girls were at school, and the weekends spent together on outings for shopping and other activities. As the girls headed into puberty and adolescence, there were a few hurdles to overcome, especially with Carol, who was still suffering with the illnesses that had been diagnosed while still at the children's home. She was often moody and silent and began staying at home alone while Veronica and Elizabeth went out together. Veronica understood, and let thing develop as they would, naturally.

When a new serious health crisis occurred, Veronica took Carol to see a doctor. As she could now afford private care, they visited a specialist with a reputation for treating such cases involving Chron's disease, and Carol underwent a new series of scans and blood tests.

The results showed that part of her intestines needed to be removed due to an infection, which posed a health risk. The doctor spoke to Veronica alone, telling her about the operation, and that her life could be at risk in the future if ever she decided to have children.

"While having Crohn's disease can influence fertility and pregnancy outcomes," the doctor explained. "Most women with Crohn's can have healthy pregnancies and births. However, active disease during pregnancy can increase the risk of complications for both mother and baby, so nothing is ever certain, and Carol will need special attention later if she decides to have children of her own."

"So should we explain this to her?" Veronica asked, slightly troubled now.

"Well, in my opinion she is still too young to be able to digest such matters properly, but during the operation we can inspect a lot of things that will help us in the future, so for the moment I think we should keep this to ourselves, if you agree…"

"Yes, of course, doctor…you know best…"

Carol was told then that a part of her intestine was badly infected by Crohn's disease and that she would have to undergo an operation to remove this and stop the risk of further infection. She appeared unalarmed at this news, and accepted it calmly, much to Veronica's relief. She knew how Carol's behaviour could become erratic at times of stress, but she presumed this was mostly because of her age, as she developed from childhood to adolescence.

A week or so later, Carol was admitted to hospital for the operation. This was carried out without undue stress, although once underway complications were discovered and the surgeon had to make a huge decision. The full examination revealed that Carol's fallopian tubes were also badly infected, and this would seriously affect her fertility cycles in later life if she decided to have children.

The surgeon paused the operation briefly and went to inform Veronica, who was in the waiting room while Carol was being operated on, of this unexpected discovery. An urgent decision was needed, and it was the mother's final prerogative to make such a decision. Taken by surprise, she felt vulnerable and panicky. What was the right decision?

"What would you recommend?" she asked the surgeon, wanting to trust his better judgement.

"Well, the safest option would be to remove the fallopian tubes to prevent further propagation, but that will mean she will never be able to have children..."

"Oh, dear...and if we leave it as it is?"

"It will only get worse, in my opinion. As I told you, these things can grow and spread if not controlled, and this is a very delicate area to be infected, especially at such a young age...my advice would be for you to grant us permission to take out all risks and make certain she can have a healthy normal life later on, apart from the infertility aspect...it's a hard decision, I understand, but it is the most advantageous for her in the long run..."

Taken short, Veronica hesitated a few moments, unsure. But she knew that Carol's whole future life could be at risk, and she couldn't live with that. She assented then, and the surgeon rushed back to complete the operation. Veronica felt dreadful deep inside, but she had had little choice. She had to go with a nurse then and sign the necessary forms that gave her authorisation for the operation, and she knew then there was no turning back, either for her or for Carol in the future. What was done was done, and the guilt blanketed Veronica's soul with no respite, even if she told herself she had probably saved her daughter's life.

She decided not to tell Carol of what had taken place, thinking her too young to be able to absorb such a devastating fact. When she was older, she would understand a lot better, or so she hoped.

Carol spent a few days in hospital recovering from the operation, and then she was allowed home to convalesce and recuperate slowly. She gradually began to feel a lot better in herself, and the operation was judged a success by the visiting doctor as she began to get up and resume a normal life. Veronica kept the awful secret she now carried alone deep in her own soul, torn between relief at her recovery and the guilt of having taken away a huge part of her life as a growing girl. She prayed that neither would live to regret it.

***

Life then returned to normal for Veronica and her daughters. Carol recovered quite well and no longer suffered as before, while Elizabeth remained a calm and reflective young teenager, attending the chapel at the convent each Sunday and talking and studying with the nuns there as much as she could. She had not renounced her intention to become a nun once she reached an age where she might enrol as a novice. Veronica let it run its course, hoping inside that the girl would change her ambitions as she grew older and made other friends outside the circle of the convent.

Veronica's publishing and editing business was doing very well, and she was busy most of the time promoting authors and new books and spreading slowly to cover a vast network across the country. It was now beyond all her first expectations, and that helped enormously while she watched her daughters go through puberty and adolescence, with both becoming attractive and sensible young ladies she could rightly feel proud of now.

Her old problem was now long gone, cast off forever, or so she told herself, and she thanked her blessings every day, knowing once again she had come through. The months turned into years, and the harmony was palpable now. That was enough for her. She had chosen a calm sense of virtue over everything else that had been thrown at her, and her daughters became the living proof of having made the correct decision.

PART TWO - DIVINITY

Chapter 14

It is easy for any family to slip into what soon becomes a complacent routine, living together in basic harmony and relying upon each other to help keep that same routine in place. There will sometimes be minor upsets and issues to resolve, of course, but most overcome these without due stress or drama.

This was now the case with Veronica and her daughters, Carol and Elizabeth, who had co-existed in almost perfect harmony and tranquillity during their teen years. So, when things took a sudden break from the routine, Veronica was taken aback somewhat, although subconsciously she had been anticipating this, if not precisely dreading it.

It started when Elizabeth turned 17 and told her mother that she felt ready to enter the convent of Sister Colette as a novice, which would entail a period of between six months and two years known as a testing period, or postulancy in the official religious language. After that period, the convent would decide if she had a true calling and vocation for the order, and she would then be accepted as a novitiate after taking temporary vows. If she persisted and adapted fully to the order's way of life, she would then be allowed to take the solemn and permanent vows as a consecrated sister of the order. A lengthy process that had been fully explained to Elizabeth by the Mother Superior over many discussions and prayers, and Elizabeth told her mother that she was ready, and this was her final choice.

Veronica accompanied Elizabeth to the convent, where they had a lengthy meeting and discussion with Sister Colette, who now felt very close to Elizabeth after following her development from child to young adult. She firmly believed that Elizabeth was ready now to join the order as a novice, and she told Veronica this.

"It is in no way definitive," she explained calmly. "And it in no way restricts Elizabeth in any future decisions she may or may not wish to make. You could consider it to be like a form of apprenticeship, I suppose, as with any other trade or livelihood in the outside world. Only Elizabeth will be able to judge for herself and know if she is ready to dedicate herself to our way of life here at the order, and so I recommend that you allow her to at least try, and we will assess her progress as she advances in our order. I'm sure that you know how passionate and ardent she has been ever since she was here as a child, and that passion has grown ever since."

And so, Veronica agreed, allowing Elizabeth to be duly indicted into the order as a novitiate a few weeks later. She had never appeared so solemn, and so happy and content, and her mother had to wipe away a few tears during the ceremony. Carol looked on with little interest, but she too had understood that changes were taking place now they were older and more independent, and she would soon be ready to put her own plans into action.

She had reached the age of eighteen, the legal age of majority, which meant that she could now take possession of the inheritance her father had left for her and her sister, and shortly after Elizabeth had left home to enter the convent, she told her mother that she would like to move into the house that was now legally hers, as she wanted to become more independent.

Veronica told her she'd think about it, feeling a little bewildered as both her daughters wanted to leave home at the same time, which meant that she would be left alone once more in her own life. It would be hard, she knew, but again, she had no right to keep them from fulfilling their own desires and living the life they chose for themselves. They had suffered enough in the past during her own turbulent period, and she felt she owed it to them to set them free and watch from afar, while being still physically close.

She told Carol then that she thought it a great idea for her to branch out on her own a little, and she would help her all she could. Her own affairs were in order and going well now, and she would have plenty of time to help both her daughters if the need ever arose.

Carol seemed pleased and relieved, and they set things in motion at once, visiting the solicitor's office that was handling the inheritance. Shortly after the official papers had been duly signed, Carol received the deeds and the keys to the house her father had left for her. The other house was in Elizabeth's name, and that would have to be dealt with separately when she also came of age. Veronica thought it best not to mention her entry into the convent until it was necessary, not wanting to involve her in anything distracting for the time being.

The house was partly furnished and in good condition, and Veronica helped Carol move into it once she had decided to do so. Together they cleaned it from top to bottom and went to buy a few things that were missing, and which Veronica thought were necessary to help Carol adjust to being alone, like a new washing machine and other kitchen implements she might need. She was like a child with a new toy as Veronica watched her drifting through the rooms slowly, as though trying to absorb the fact that this was *her* home now, and she could do as she wished in it.

"Are you sure you'll be all right living here on your own?" she asked then, like any concerned mother watching her children quit the nest.

"I think so, yes," Carol told her firmly. "I have my job at the supermarket, and I think I'll soon have saved enough to pass my driving test and get a small car to get around in."

"Well, that will be nice for you," Veronica smiled, happy that she sounded so positive. "You'll be able to get and about a bit then and make lots of new friends…"

"Yes…I do miss Elizabeth a lot now she's gone…"

"So do I," Veronica told her. "But I'm sure she's happy doing what she is now."

"Yes, so do I. It's all she spoke about most of the time lately. Even her friends at school used to call her the little nun in the playground!"

They both laughed at this joke, but now they knew how serious Elizabeth's devotion and determination was.

And so, Veronica found herself once again alone in her home, leaving Carol to start her own independent life, although she felt confident that she would manage. She had been a solitary child from the start, often preferring to sit alone and stare into the distance, and her illness had intensified this during a time. But now she appeared happy and excited, and Veronica felt certain that things would go smoothly for all of them from now on. And she was there, close and available, feeling once again like a true mother. Her daughters knew that as well.

Chapter 15

Elizabeth had been at the convent for about six months when Carol moved into her own house, and she'd had little contact with her mother or sister during the initiation stage of her induction. She had taken the name of Sister Angelina and was soon quite at ease with convent life and the community of nuns surrounding her. She sometimes helped in the children's-home part of the convent, being experienced from her own short stay there several years previously. She was popular and liked by all the staff and children, while recalling her own tribulations which had led, inadvertently, to her being there now as a novitiate.

One morning, the Mother Superior summoned her to her office, wanting to ask about her initial sejour at the convent and if she had any issues with her vocation.

"Everything is fine," she replied with a smile and a soft voice. "I feel that this is my rightful place in the world, and I enjoy the company as well as the silence of prayer and devotion we all share every day."

"I am pleased to hear that," Sister Colette replied. "Even as a child here you did strike me as being rather different, and now I know why. I think you will soon be ready for a full initiation into the order, and then you can decide which direction you would like your life here to take."

"Thank you, Mother Superior. I look forward to that."

"Good. But now I would like you to take up a position in the kitchens, as there is a vacancy, and it is good for all our novitiates to experience every aspect of our life here."

"Of course, I understand. And thank you for thinking of me…"

"That is good then, and may God bless you and may your commitment to Jesus be all-rewarding…"

"Thank you, Mother."

She went to the kitchen then and met with Sister Marie, who ran and organised the cooking of meals for the nuns. They knew each other, of course, and Sister Marie welcomed her with a broad smile.

"Welcome to my domain!" she chuckled, wiping her hands on a tea-towel.

"Thank you," Elizabeth replied. "I hope I will be up to the new position…"

"Oh, I'm sure you will be. It isn't difficult or complicated, but we do have a strict timetable to uphold, as you know, with our different prayer times and meals, but I'm sure you'll soon get the hang of it…"

She wanted to do well in this new position, as she had in all the work and service she had undertaken since joining the order, serving the Lord in the way that she loved.

Sister Marie had become a nun late in life, when she was around forty. She had worked most of her life in the catering industry and had been a head chef in a large hotel when she felt herself called towards a religious life. She had always been a churchgoer, and though her calling was later than usual, she knew she must see it through.

Once accepted and ordained, the Mother Superior had asked her to take over the running of the kitchen, as the nun who had been in charge was about to retire due to her advanced age, and she readily agreed. It appeared to be her calling, even in such different surroundings, and she submitted humbly and with inner joy.

Elizabeth – now Sister Angelina – soon fell into the rhythm of the kitchen and fulfilled her duties with care and a merry disposition, which the other nuns working with her appreciated and often commented on.

"It's like having the sun shining in here with us, even when it's cold and wet outside…"

"Yes, that's true…our very own little angel from heaven, humming and singing away to make all our chores seem like nothing…"

"God has certainly blessed our kitchen, anyway, and even our food tastes better now at every meal…"

"Oh, do stop!" Elizabeth begged them with a smile. "You're making me blush redder than this beetroot I'm peeling and cutting up…"

And so, she worked and smiled and hummed her way through her chores, interspersed with prayers and services in the chapel. She had never felt more content and fulfilled, she was certain about that, and never once doubted or regretted her decision to become a nun. It felt as though the outside world and all its daily problems had been cast aside, and the convent was her own world now. She often thought about her mother and older sister, though. They could never be forgotten, as she well knew.

***

During her early days in the kitchen, she noticed that the same delivery man came two or three times each week, bringing all the vegetables and other products necessary to prepare the simple meals the convent served to its residents. He always had a cheerful aspect about him and chatted non-stop with the kitchen staff, who knew him well enough to enjoy his banter.

Elizabeth felt intrigued and always watched him with a keen eye when she thought he wasn't looking at her. She had had little contact with the opposite sex while growing up, obsessed as she was with the idea of becoming a nun, and the usual teenage boy/girl friendships had remained foreign to her. But this man seemed to catch her attention now, and it troubled her a little.

And then one day when she happened to be alone in the kitchen, he introduced himself to her with a grin.

"Hello, I'm Sidney Harding, but most people just call me Sid. You're new here, aren't you, Sister?"

"Yes, I've been at the convent for a few months now, and I started working in the kitchen a few weeks ago. I'm pleased to meet you, Sid…"

"And it's nice to meet you as well. May I ask your name?"

"Oh, of course. I am Sister Angelina."

"That's a pretty name...like after the angels, eh? Well, I deliver all your vegetables and things here two or three times a week, so you'll be seeing me a lot..."

"Yes, I had noticed..."

"That's nice. Don't suppose you could make me a cup of tea, could you? The other Sisters always do when I have time..."

"Oh, of course...they're all at Chapel this morning for a special service and so they left me to look after the kitchen for a while..."

She made him tea and took note of his friendly attitude. He looked to be in his late twenties, perhaps, although she was hard pressed to put any age upon him, due to her lack of experience with adult men. But she couldn't help but notice how much he looked at her while chatting, and it made her feel a little uncomfortable after a time. Is that what men did when alone with a young woman?

He finished his tea and then made ready to leave. She felt a little relieved.

" I have a lot more deliveries to make, so I must be going now," he told her. "But I'll probably see you again next week if you're still here in the kitchen. Goodbye, Sister Angelina..."

"Goodbye, Sid. God bless you..."

Over the following weeks it became a regular occurrence for Elizabeth to make Sid a cup of tea during his deliveries, which inevitably led them to chatting a little while she carried on with her kitchen duties. The other Sisters noticed this and nudged each other in a playful manner. Elizabeth herself was noticing more how he seemed always to single her out, and when she happened to be absent from the kitchen during his visits her colleagues always told her how he'd asked after her whereabouts. This began to trouble her a little, and she worried that she was growing too close to him without realising it.

Once when they were alone in the kitchen and he was enjoying the tea she'd made for him, he asked why she wanted to become a nun.

"I don't know how to explain it, really," she told him. "I had a calling from Jesus I think when I was still a young child, and I've followed that calling as I grew up. But I don't really want to discuss any of that, nor my past life, so I'd be grateful if you didn't ask questions about it..."

"Oh, I do apologise," he said, a little shamefaced. "I didn't mean to upset you, really...I think I'm just a little bit too nosey..."

"It doesn't matter, so don't worry about it," she smiled. "It's just quite a difficult period for us when we first begin this way of life, and so much is uncertain, you understand?"

"Yes, of course I do..."

But she felt rather troubled after he'd gone, and she couldn't stop thinking about him and his questions, wondering if she should do anything about it. She even toyed with the idea of talking with the Mother Superior about her feelings, but she still couldn't admit to herself that she was feeling attracted to this man. She decided to keep her feelings to herself for the present and wait to see how it all developed, if at all.

And then one day Sid came to the convent without delivering his usual wares, and Elizabeth happened to be alone in the kitchen. She was surprised and a little embarrassed.

"It's not your delivery day today, is it?" she questioned.

"Er, no...but I was delivering close-by and so I decided to visit you anyway. I hope you don't mind?"

"Well, no, we're not very busy right now...it is a bit strange for me though, to be truthful. You know we're not allowed to have personal visitors while in the novitiate stage..."

"Oh, no, I didn't know, sorry...."

"Well, no harm done, as the others aren't here right now. But I would ask you not to do it again."

"Of course, don't worry. But may I be open with you a little now that I'm here?"

"Yes, why not?"

"Well, I must confess that I feel a very strong attraction towards you now, and I find it difficult to stay away from you..."

"Oh, dear, really? I don't know what to say," she told him, trying to remain calm. "You do understand that I'm in the process of becoming a fully ordained nun, don't you?"

"Yes, I do. And I will understand if you ask me to leave and never come back and talk alone with you, truly. I just wanted you to know about my true feelings, that's all. I find you very attractive as a young woman..."

"Thank you," she murmured softly, knowing deep inside that she felt the same attraction towards him, but determined not to allow it to surface. "But I am totally committed to my vows, so I think we must avoid being alone together from now on…"

"Yes, of course, if that's what you really want. But I sincerely hope you might change your mind one day, and then I will become the happiest man in the world, really…"

They looked hard into each other's eyes a moment, and they both felt something pass between them, one of those invisible clouds that carry messages to yearning hearts when words are totally inadequate. Elizabeth felt a panic arising in her breast and was about to turn and run away when the kitchen door opened and Sister Marie entered with a smile.

"Ah, hello, Sid!" she said. "We weren't expecting you today, were we?"

"Er, no, Sister…I forgot to leave something last time and so I popped it in quick as I was close by…" Sid stammered.

"Oh?"

"Yes," Elizabeth said quickly, grabbing a closed packet of seasoning herbs lying on a table. "I needed this for today's ragout…"

"That's good then…thank you, Sid. We'll see you next week then?"

"Yes, of course…goodbye, Sisters…"

He dashed out, a little unsettled, but glad that Elizabeth had covered for him so rapidly. Could she possibly feel the same way about him as he did about her? He felt his heart beating with a faint hope again.

***

Sid had married when he was just eighteen, while the girl he married, Dorothy, was only sixteen. School sweethearts, they had begun intimate relations very early, and like so many of their generation, they discovered one day that Dorothy was pregnant. Still madly in love with one another, they decided to get married and raise the child as a couple, with the blessings of both families.

To begin with they were very happy, leaving their respective family homes and moving together into a rented flat. Soon after, Dorothy gave birth to a baby girl whom they named Kim. Their marriage appeared to be going very well, and they were truly very happy together.

Once the baby had grown into a toddler and could attend a day nursery, Dorothy found a job as a seamstress at a fashion house, where she seemed happy and was getting on very well. Sid was also making his own way in his working life and had a good position with a large distribution company that supplied fruit and vegetables to various institutions, including schools, hospitals, and even a convent, as we have already learnt.

After a year or two, he decided that's what he wanted to do in a more serious manner and so decided to start his own business. By his early twenties he had built up quite a steady business, with contracts to supply and deliver fruit and vegetables and other commodities to some of the local supermarkets, as well as the many other institutions he already knew. It seemed a perfect life for them both and their daughter, and they were prospering as a happily married couple.

But over time, Sid had become so tied up with the running of his business that he began to neglect his family life somewhat, leaving home early in the morning and returning late at night, and Dorothy began to feel a little surplus to his needs. Kim was growing into a charming little girl, sweet and pretty and the apple of both her parents' eyes, but it was falling more onto Dorothy to look after her, especially when she started school, and she too noticed how her father, whom she adored, was more often absent while working all hours of the day and night. A new tension crept into their lives, although Sid mostly ignored it, intent only on his business and giving his family a decent lifestyle.

Dorothy was still working at the fashion house, and she noticed that the head of the enterprise, James Walker, was paying a lot of attention towards her, often praising her work and stopping to chat with her, much to the amusement of her fellow workers, who began teasing her about being the boss's pet. She felt flattered by this attention, because she knew that she was still a very attractive young woman, despite being married and with a child to look after, and having been married very young she often felt she'd missed out on her teenage years, when all her friends had been out enjoying themselves and flirting endlessly with different boys before getting married and settling down.

She felt a new aura of desire creeping into her soul, and to have so much attention paid to her by the head of the fashion house was a warming sensation that let her know that men were still attracted to her, while Sid, her husband, whom she dearly loved, seemed to be ignoring her and her inner needs, always tied up with his business affairs and ignoring her own desires, claiming he was too tired or too busy.

James Walker, her boss, knew of course that she was married, but he still felt attracted to her, and he knew that she liked him a lot in much the same way. And so, inevitably, things got more intense, and they started dating on different occasions after work, while Sid remained oblivious of anything untoward. If he came home and found a babysitter looking after Kim and Dorothy not at home, he was told that she'd gone out with some of the girls at work, and so he didn't mind. She was still young and needed to go out sometimes, and he knew that he was away from home far too much, but his business still took priority.

This went on for some months, and eventually Sid started to notice subtle changes in Dorothy's behaviour towards him. At weekends, when he was at home, she tended to avoid any closeness with him, whereas before they were a touchy-feely couple still very much in love. Now she made excuses, and often went out on her own, shopping, she said, or meeting some girlfriend or other for a coffee and a chat, while leaving Kim at home with him, saying it was time he looked after his daughter sometimes. He felt a little bewildered but was too tired to argue or think anything bad of it. He thought she would grow out of it eventually.

And he did enjoy being with Kim, who was a delightful companion now for him. They often went out together to various attractions, and the girl was delighted to be alone with him, as she knew he would always spoil her rotten and give in to all her demands. Little clouds of happiness, but which didn't let him see the storm clouds that were gathering around him and his family and that would soon burst and bring chaos to his almost-perfect life.

Things came to a head one Saturday when Sid was walking through the shopping centre with Kim, heading for her favourite toyshop. As they passed by the food area where the cafés and restaurants were as busy as always at lunchtime, Sid suddenly came to a halt and stared open-mouthed towards one of the better restaurants. He had spotted Dorothy, who was supposed to be out with a group of her girlfriends from work. She was sitting at a table with a man, whom he quickly recognised as her boss, James Walker, and they were sharing a meal and drinking wine from crystal glasses. But what most surprised and rankled Sid was the way they were holding hands over the table, staring lovingly at one another like first-time teenagers on a date. And when they leaned towards each other and shared a warm kiss, he felt his heart plunging to depths he didn't know existed.

Kim was surprised by her father's abrupt stop, but he quickly recovered his wits and pulled her away before she saw her mother sitting at the restaurant with a strange man. He hurried her off to the toy shop where he allowed her to browse and choose whatever took her fancy, as though suddenly indifferent to her caprices and demands. This also surprised her, but in a pleasant way. It felt like her birthday and Christmas rolled into one in her young thoughts.

Sid was a very calm person by nature. He'd never once questioned Dorothy's love for him and their life together, but now he felt his mind in turmoil. How long had this been going on? Was her love just a sham then, a pretence that had played out for him as and when it suited her? He felt betrayed, and rather foolish, having understood in a single glance the pretence he'd been living in for maybe longer than he could calculate. And that hurt a great deal.

The confrontation occurred that same evening, when Kim was in bed in her room and Dorothy returned home, smiling and slightly tipsy.

"Everything all right?" she asked, kissing him briefly on the cheek.

"No, not really," he replied with a stern look in his eye.

"What's wrong?"

"I saw you today, in the restaurant…"

Her face crumpled, and she knew that he had guessed, or knew.

"Oh, dear," she mumbled, confused. "I am sorry…"

There was no huge row nor any fighting. Sid remained calm and factual. If she preferred the other man over him, that was her choice. But he couldn't go on sharing a life with her, and she would have to accept and understand that. She told him that she did. Something had broken inside him, and he felt wounded and vulnerable, but he wouldn't dwell on it or throw reproaches at her. That wasn't his way.

He arranged to rent a flat and moved out shortly after. She agreed that they would share custody of Kim, and they were divorced some months later. Dorothy moved in with James, and that was the end of Sid's married life. His business took over his life even more then. And some considerable time after all this, he had met Sister Angelina at the convent, better known to him now as Elizabeth.

***

Elizabeth wasn't sure how to handle the situation that she felt growing around her now at the convent. Sid was visiting a lot more than usual, and she felt it was becoming a little beyond her control. She did feel a strange new attraction towards the man, and on one occasion, when he kissed her briefly on the cheek on leaving, she experienced a sensation deep inside which was completely unknown to her, and she knew she would like to explore it further. Never having known such things while growing up, she told herself that it must be what love felt like. But she knew that if she were to fall in love with him, she would be obliged to renounce her sacred vows and leave the convent, and she really didn't want that to happen.

After a few weeks of this double life of prayer and doubt and hesitation, she decided that she must speak with the Mother Superior and let her know what was happening in her thoughts. She knew it was unfair to the other Sisters with whom she shared her life, and she was being unfaithful, at least in thought, to Jesus and the vows she had already taken to serve him and him alone, and this gave rise to a host of new feelings of guilt.

"I have something I want to confess," she told the Mother Superior.

"Oh, dear," Sister Colette replied, a little worried. "I hope it's nothing too serious?"

"Well, I think it might be," Elizabeth went on. "You see, I've been feeling quite a strong attraction towards the man who delivers to the kitchen every week, and I think he feels the same towards me."

"Well, that could seem quite alarming, I suppose," the Mother Superior went on. "Although in the outside world it is a normal occurrence, as you must know. How did this start, if I may ask?"

"I don't really know," Elizabeth confessed, blushing a little now. "He just began talking a lot with me, and I enjoyed that. Then he would come to see me when I was alone in the kitchen and talk with me, and I found I was enjoying the attention. It just grew from that, I think…"

"Yes, I see. Do the other Sisters in the kitchen know about this?"

"I don't think so, Mother. I haven't told anyone."

"Good. Well, I can only advise you as best I can, although I must tell you that you're not the first novice postulant who has undergone such feelings, so don't feel any guilt or shame about it."

"I am sorry, Mother, but I feel as though I've let you down a little, and the whole Sisterhood. And it makes me think that I should perhaps leave the convent and try to make a new life for myself in the outside world…"

"I do understand," Sister Colette continued calmly. "But you must think very hard about this. I wouldn't want you to make the wrong decision and then have to live with doubts and regrets. So, let's wait a while and see how things develop, shall we, while you meditate and pray and think deeply about what you really want to do with your life. And please try to do this calmly while remembering the vows you took on entering our order. You are not the first to have doubts, as I have already told you, and it is perfectly normal for girls of your age to have such feelings, truly."

"All right, Mother. I will try to come to terms with all this as calmly as I can. But it's all so unexpected, it's taken me rather by surprise..."

"Yes, I can see that. But don't worry, whatever you decide you will have my full backing, so you must think things through and decide in your own time and conscience. Your prayers will help you, I feel certain, and God will watch over you whatever you may decide..."

Elizabeth left the office then, still a little confused but feeling a lot more confident after talking with the Mother Superior. Her own mother was now absent from her life, as well as her only sister, and it was daunting to have to face all this by herself. But she still felt protected by the prayers and the work she lived with in the convent, and she hoped that would be enough to see her make the right decisions.

Over the following days and weeks, she continued her normal life at the convent, working daily in the kitchen and following the prayer services and meditations as before. But there was always a nagging doubt accompanying her now, and Sid's constant visits didn't help. She felt deep inside that her choice had already been made, although she continued to question her true feelings and motivations.

Sid visited more often, and she slowly learned his life story through his conversations. He was divorced with one daughter named Kim. He ran his own business and had bought a new house recently. Elizabeth was reluctant to tell him her own history, believing it might influence him in a wrong way. He told her she was mysterious, but he enjoyed that idea. He really wanted them to be together eventually and learn to love each other over time. She respected him for that idea, as he respected her own hesitations and beliefs.

Her resistance was slowly worn away, but naturally. Sid knew how devout she was and insisted he would always respect her beliefs. But he loved her deeply and hoped she would agree to marry him eventually and raise a family. She told him she was still unsure but would be willing to at least consider a future together.

Shortly after this she decided to leave the convent, and Sid understood that she would come to live with him, and that they would be married as soon as it could be arranged. There was no mention of her family, and Sid presumed this was how she wanted things to be. Their love would be enough to see them through, he felt certain.

Chapter 16

Carol, meanwhile, was still working at her local supermarket. From being a cashier at the checkout tills she had been promoted to sales assistant in the electrical department, which she found more interesting as she met a lot of different people. The manager had spotted her potential to become part of the management team and so had promoted her without hesitation. Her role included providing customers with information on electrical products as well as selling them. She quickly formed a technique that helped achieve her goal of becoming an independent salesperson without relying on any manager.

She soon become quite friendly with a few of her colleagues, and on some evenings after work they would visit a local pub together and have a meal and a drink. She enjoyed such outings and looked forward to these evenings spent with her colleagues. They would discuss and talk about their families and husbands and children, and Carol felt herself a little isolated then, having lived alone for so long already. She did sometimes mention her childhood, her mother's 'illnesses', and how she and her sister had spent some time in a convent children's home, while the others listened with compassion.

But mostly it was great fun for her to mix with other people, although she didn't realise right off that she was sometimes drinking a lot more than she ought to, but she didn't worry too much about that. She found that she was enjoying herself by mixing with other people, and sometimes they would attend karaoke evenings, where she loved to join in and sing. When she first started singing, everyone told her that she had a great voice, and that made her very happy. She also managed to stave off the loneliness she sometimes felt, mixing with these friends from work who were mostly married with families, and that increased the craving she often felt to have her own family life and fulfilment.

One of the managers from the supermarket, a young, single man named Mark, would sometimes join the others on their pub visits, and after a while he began speaking to and showing a particular interest in Carol, whom he knew to be single and unattached. She found this attention flattering, and when one day at work he eventually asked her to go out alone with him for a meal, she gladly accepted, laughing off her colleagues' suggestions and innuendos during the rest of that day. She knew it was simply playful banter, but she also knew deep down that this invitation was all she'd been wanting for a very long time now.

Their first outing together was very pleasant, and Carol realised that he was serious in his intentions towards her. Her own loneliness diminished as they went out alone together more often, and they began talking about the future and what their separate dreams held in common. Then one evening when they were in a group from work at a karaoke evening, Mark proposed to her, and presented her with a fabulous engagement ring.

Struck speechless for a few moments, she gazed deeply into his eyes, and the sincerity she saw there made up her mind for her, despite both being a little merry from the drinking they'd indulged in. She accepted his proposal, and a great cheer rose up from their work colleagues while a bottle of champagne was ordered. A noisy toast followed, and some bright spark put the well-known song 'Get me to the church on time...' on the karaoke player, with the whole group joining in with full voice. It was a very merry evening indeed, and the next day Carol really believed she had found her life's happiness at last.

The following day Carol called her mother, Veronica, to give her the news about her engagement to Mark. They had grown closer ever since her sister Elizabeth had joined the convent and abandoned a normal life, and now Veronica felt delighted for her eldest daughter, although certain dark shadows still blighted her own conscience. But she brushed those thoughts aside and congratulated Carol with all her love.

"He's someone who works with you at the supermarket, then?" she asked.

"Yes, one of the managers. I've been going out with him for some time now, and he really is a lovely man. You'll have to meet him when you have time."

"I'd like that, yes. We should let Elizabeth know as well, if you think you'll be getting married one day..."

"Yes, that would be nice, all of us together again. Have you heard from her lately?"

"No, I haven't," Veronica told her. "But I suppose she's so tied up with her life at the convent she has no time to think about us and life outside anymore."

Yes," Carol agreed. "I haven't had a word since she left home..."

"Well, you could always call the convent and speak with her, if you want, and let her know your good news. I'm sure she'll be delighted, as I am…"

"All right, I will. And we must get together when you have time. I'd like to make some alterations at the house and maybe get some new furniture and things…"

"Ah, so you plan to live their when you are married, then?"

"Yes, of course. It is a nice place, and it would be lovely to raise my own family there, don't you think?"

"Er…yes, I suppose so," Veronica stuttered as the old haunting shadows reappeared. "So let me know when you are free and we can meet…"

"All right, I will. And you can meet Mark at the same time…"

"Lovely…look forward to it…"

Carol called the convent the following day and asked to speak with her sister, Elizabeth, now known as Sister Angelina. The Mother Superior seemed surprised at first, and Carol thought that she'd perhaps forgotten who she was.

"I'm Carol, her sister," she explained.

"Yes, of course, I do know who you are," Sister Colette replied. "How are things going now for you? And your mother?"

"We're both fine, thank you. My mother is still running her publishing business and it's doing very well, and I'm working in management at one of the big stores and have just become engaged to get married, and so I wanted to tell Elizabeth about it...."

"She hasn't been in touch with you then..."

"No, not at all, actually, ever since she joined your convent..."

"Well, that is peculiar. You see, she decided to leave us after a few months, as she also met a young man and decided she wanted to get married as well...I'm really surprised she hasn't contacted you about this..."

Carol felt bewildered on hearing this news and didn't know how to respond. They had drifted apart, certainly, over the intervening years, but she hadn't thought it was so striking. Had Elizabeth decided then to drift away on her own and live her life as she thought fit? It was strange, to say the least.

"When did she leave the convent?" she asked.

"Oh, a few weeks ago now. As I said, she got to know the man who delivers to our kitchen. His name is Sidney Harding, and I think they felt attracted to each other from the start. She spoke to me a lot about the situation and her own feelings, and in the end, she decided that she'd rather live in the outside world than here in the convent as a fully inducted Sister. I advised her to follow her heart, which she eventually did."

"But did she tell you where she was going? I mean, do you have a forwarding address?"

"Well, no, she didn't, actually...I'm sorry. But I think she had the intention of marrying Sid and living with him eventually. He still comes here once a week to deliver, so I could ask him and let him know that you would like to speak with her."

"Okay, thank you…"

Carol explained the situation to her mother, and they both thought it odd that Elizabeth hadn't contacted them to let them know about the changes in her life. Veronica had really believed that she would become a fully-fledged nun and spend her life in prayer and devotion, but she had obviously changed her mind. Deep down, she felt a little relieved about this, and hoped it would be better for her future happiness in life. If both her daughters were to be married, she also felt hopeful in herself that she might eventually know the joys of becoming a grandmother, despite doubts and fears that dwelt in dark corners of her own mind. The past always lingered, deep down, and she knew it would never disappear entirely.

When Carol decided to hold an engagement party at her home, she tried calling the number given to her by the Mother Superior but could get no reply. She presumed that the man with whom Elizabeth had decided to share her life with had changed his number for some reason. After a few fruitless searches on the internet, she and her mother accepted that Elizabeth had decided to remain isolated in her own life, no matter what she undertook. Sadly, they took this in and hoped that sometime in the future contact would be somehow resumed.

The engagement party went well, and Veronica was pleased to meet Mark, the man who was to become her first daughter's husband. At the same time, she found herself looking back over the years that seemed to have passed so quickly, and how all their lives had been turned around, mostly for the better. She felt the absence of Elizabeth quite keenly, but knew she would be in her thoughts, no matter where she might be now. She prayed inwardly that she too was happy in her own choices.

Carol and Mark were married a few months after the engagement party. It was a small affair, mostly with work colleagues attending along with a few of Mark's closest relatives. Both Veronica and Carol had tried to contact Elizabeth, but without success, sadly. They would have both loved her to be with them on such a special day, and it was a constant nagging worry not knowing where she was and if she was happy in her new chosen life.

The wedding took place at the local Catholic Church. The priest was friendly, and they asked for the choir to be present to sing a few hymns. Mark visited his tailor and had a new suit made, while Carol had also been measured for a custom-made wedding dress, in which she looked splendid and happy. Veronica felt very proud to see her daughter dressed in such a way, and she couldn't stop a stray tear or two as the bride walked down the aisle on the arm of a friend from work. If only her father could have seen her, she thought to herself, but brushed away such thoughts. The past was done with, she knew.

After the ceremony, they posed for a few photographs and then went with Veronica and a small group to a local restaurant, where a special meal had been reserved. It was a pleasant afternoon and evening, still small-scale but more than enough for the newlywed couple, who were to begin their new life together properly now. This meant such a lot to both.

Eager to be alone, they took leave of family and friends and took a taxi home.

"Happy?" Mark asked as they were whisked away.

"Oh, yes," Carol replied with a huge smile. "Happier than I've ever been…"

They kissed, and so began their new life, sealed with a special knowledge that seemed unbreakable on the first night.

Chapter 17

Mark and Carol were happy together for the first few months of their marriage, sharing the many new and different aspects of their combined lives. They had decided early on that they wanted to raise a family together, but as the weeks turned into months and nothing seemed to be happening, they started questioning this lack of results.

Believing it could be a problem on his side, Mark underwent a private testing at specialised clinic. The results showed that he had a high sperm count and there were no other issues preventing him from fathering children.

When he told Carol about the test results, she agreed to go for tests herself, to find out if there might be a problem on her side. She scheduled a visit to her local doctor, who examined her quite thoroughly and then told her that she should have further tests at the fertility clinic at the hospital. She was quite disturbed by this, wondering then what the problem could be, although she realised right then that the problem was indeed on her side.

Mark, too, seemed preoccupied by this when she told him, although he tried to be comforting and reassuring, telling her that he was certain they'd get to the cause of the problem and fix it. She wanted to believe him, although shadowy doubts crept into her own thoughts as she vaguely recalled her health problems from her younger days.

After numerous examinations and deep scans, she received the news a week or so later that she was unable to have children, due to an operation she had undergone some years ago which had been linked to a serious illness that had dogged her childhood and early teens, and which had most probably saved her life at the time. Vague memories flooded back into her mind, memories she had doggedly rejected as she'd grown up, but suddenly it all came back to her: her mother's alcoholism, the convent care home, her sickness and hospitalisation, and the operation she'd undergone almost with indifference. Now, she felt horrified, and quite alarmed. What had been done to her without her knowledge? And who was to blame?

She reluctantly told Mark about the results she'd received from the hospital, and she watched his expression change as he read the damning notes and diagnosis. She felt a cloud of guilt growing around her, even though she hadn't known anything about it when she'd agreed to marry him. But would he understand that? His frowning face made her fear the worst.

"I hope this won't make any difference to our relationship?" she said softly.

He looked hard at her, as though trying to fathom something out, and he didn't answer her straight off, lost in thought and looking disappointed.

"I suppose we'll just have to accept the situation," he said eventually with a sigh. "We could always try to adopt a child sometime in the future…although that wouldn't be the same as having our own child…"

"No, it wouldn't," she replied abruptly, as though shocked by this idea. "I'm sorry, Mark, but I don't think I could go through with that idea…"

He just stared hard at her again and then told her that he was going out to the pub to have a drink with some of his friends. Her heart sank as he put on his coat and left, slamming the front door as he went. She felt it to be another form of protest against such damning news, for which she knew she was culpable. She broke down into tears then, finding herself suddenly alone with a burden of guilt she didn't know how to handle. All she wanted was for him to be happy as she became pregnant and they waited together for their first child, as they been planning for some time. Now it appeared that the whole dream lay in ruins, and they would never know the joys they'd been preparing for.

The following day she visited her mother, Veronica, and told her about the situation, and how she'd undergone tests that revealed she was unable to have children. She asked her then if she knew anything about this and wanted details about the operation she'd undergone as a child while ill at the children's home. Veronica looked a little flustered then but tried to reassure her by saying that she was sure everything would work out all right eventually if they kept trying for a child.

"But why would they tell me that I can't ever have children?" Carol insisted, sensing that her mother knew more than she was letting on.

"I shouldn't worry too much about that, Carol," her mother told her. "They often get things wrong, you know, so just try to put it out of your mind and get on with your life normally. I'm sure you'll have children one day."

Carol was hardly convinced. She knew her mother well enough by now to know that she was hiding something from her, but she decided not to push it further just then. There were other ways of discovering the truth, and she left her mother to steep in her own guilt and disillusions while returning home to Mark and her own now uncertain future with him.

Over the coming weeks, Carol noticed how Mark's attitude towards her was changing. He began blaming her for their not having children, and was out most nights drinking with friends, often staying out until the early hours of the morning, when he thought her to be asleep. She wasn't, though, and stayed awake until she heard him coming in, usually quite drunk, and then she pretended to be asleep to avoid any argument or conflict he might begin on the subject. She was far from happy now and could see no easy solution.

She quickly became the victim of a severe depression, which in turn led to her drinking a lot more than she usually did. Her inability to conceive and have children appeared to be impacting them both quite severely now, and they were both drinking too much on their own side and becoming hostile and aggressive when together.

Mark told Carol then that he thought she was drinking too much and should look after her health, if she really did want to conceive and have children. But he continued staying out late and drinking alone or with a group of friends, worsening their already troubled relationship. He began staying with friends then, blaming Carol's intolerable behaviour.

Carol's mental balance appeared to be taking a turn for the worse, and she was soon suffering with a serious depression, often staying in bed until the afternoon. She was adversely affected by her excessive drinking, quickly resulting in a total loss of self-control. Mark noticed all this and became quite worried, not really considering his own actions towards her were to blame. He knew the fact that she was considered infertile had really knocked her happiness and self-belief out of the picture, while he himself now struggled to handle it all.

He went with her to the General Hospital in search for some kind of help. After an emergency assessment, the hospital recommended that Carol contact her G.P. who would prescribe certain medication to help her with her depression, and then she was allowed home. Carol realised then that she needed to change her behaviour if she wanted to save her marriage, knowing that her current path was unsustainable. Mark still struggled to understand everything that contributed to Carol's depression and found it increasingly difficult to cope with her hysteria and silent episodes, feeling that she was blaming him, and him alone.

Veronica, Carol's mother, visited her at home shortly after this, and she noticed at once that her daughter wasn't her normal cheerful self and wasn't looking after her home or her own well-being. She knew all the tell-tale signs of over-drinking from her own experiences in the distant past, and the appearance of her daughter alarmed her and told her that things weren't good.

Slowly, as Carol opened up to her a little, she learned that Mark and herself had been arguing a great deal since her diagnosis, and now Mark was mostly absent, drinking with work colleagues and staying with friends, often leaving Carol alone. She feared their marriage was breaking down irretrievably, and she felt it was her fault because of her inability to conceive. Mark was just a normal husband who wanted to raise a family with his wife. She couldn't comply with his wishes, so he was absent.

"That's not good," Veronica told her. "I'll try to contact him and find out why he doesn't come home."

"Thanks, mum…"

"But are you sure you'll be all right on your own now?"

"Yes, don't worry about me, I'll be fine," Carol told her.

"Well, I'm here if you need me," Veronica told her, worried. "You can always come and stay with me if you feel like it, until this is all sorted out."

"That won't be necessary, really, mum. I'm sure he'll come back soon…"

"I hope so…I don't like to see you in such a state, really…"

Worrying about Carol also had a negative effect upon Veronica, having realised that she was drinking a lot, which only increased problems, as she well knew from experience. She was also worried about Elizabeth and still didn't understand why she had chosen to abandon her family. All this caused the situation with Carol to appear far worse than it probably was, and Veronica found herself tempted at one point to have a drink to steady her wayward nerves. But she quickly dismissed this idea and thought better of it. It was quite alarming though, as she hadn't had that notion in a very long time.

Veronica got to see Mark shortly after this, meeting him after work before he went off drinking with his colleagues. They went to a quiet café and had a coffee together. Mark guessed the reason for this meeting, as if he'd almost been expecting it. He knew how close Carol was to her mother.

"It's good to see you again," he told her. "How are you?"

"I'm fine, but I am concerned a bit about Carol…"

"Yes, I know," he said, looking grim. "It is a terrible situation, to be honest."

"Well, may I ask you something, Mark? I mean, I don't want you to think that I'm interfering or anything, but she was really upset when I visited her the other day and I was wondering if you could explain things a bit for me, from your side, that is?"

"So, what do you want to know?"

"Carol said that you've been avoiding her a lot lately, and that you only went home rarely nowadays, so you can imagine how that makes her feel, can't you?"

"Yes, of course I do, but I don't like to see her in the condition she gets herself into now, drinking too much and ignoring me when I do go home. I can't see much of a future for us now, after her medical tests showed that she can't conceive and have children normally, and I think that's the main reason she started drinking…"

Veronica remained quiet, fully understanding the seriousness of their circumstances while recognising that they needed to address it independently. She felt her own sense of guilt rising again, that operation she'd agreed to when Carol was still so young and unable to make her own decisions, and she knew that she was in part to blame for this new set of circumstances that threatened her marriage to Mark and her life with him in the future now.

She wanted to be able to tell him the truth, letting him know that she was to blame for Carol's situation, and not her. But she couldn't muster the courage. She knew it wouldn't help anyway, only upset things even more. So, she said nothing, and hoped that Mark would find a way to solve the issue without breaking up their marriage. More, she was unable to do. She left him then, knowing she had failed in her wish to help Carol, although he did agree to visit Carol and try to talk things through with her.

He arranged to meet Carol in a local restaurant, where they had a meal and a bottle of wine, mostly in silence. They had agreed to meet and discuss their circumstances and possible future together, but Mark was reluctant to talk about any of that once sitting opposite her. Every time she questioned him on his intentions towards her, he changed the subject and talked about his own life and his friends. It wasn't precisely aggressive in character, but she felt at once that he wasn't interested in her any longer, nor in their sharing a home and a life.

She found Mark's attitude strange and almost cruel, and she refused his offer to drive her home when they eventually left the restaurant. She knew he'd had too much to drink, so she took a taxi home.

"See you," Mark muttered as a goodbye.

Carol didn't bother to reply. She had a lot of thinking to do, and she wondered why he'd taken her out for a meal in the first place. She questioned whether it had been a final goodbye on his part, and when she started to think about her marriage to him, she had to ask herself whether they had anything in common at all now things had turned sour. She sensed that her marriage was nearing its end, as he no longer showed any interest in her or her life.

She telephoned to her mother to say that she was back home and that nothing had been achieved after meeting with Mark. She thanked her for arranging the meeting anyway. Veronica asked if she could call round to see her, and Carol agreed. She needed a friendly face to look at and a friendly word to comfort her.

When she arrived at the house, she saw at once how distraught Carol was. She kissed her on the cheek and held her tightly.

"I can see you're upset," she said. "I suppose things didn't go smoothly with Mark?"

"Thanks for coming, Mum. I know I can always rely on you, and I need your support now. With everything going on with Mark and other things I feel a bit overwhelmed."

"What happened then?"

"Well, I think my marriage with Mark is over. We don't seem able to get on at all now ever since I found out I can't give him the child he wants so badly. He's like a different person now, and to be honest I think he's found somebody else. He hardly spoke with me at the restaurant and couldn't wait to get away. He drank a lot as well and became quite aggressive…"

Veronica seemed surprised at this. She'd expected Mark to at least explain his views to Carol in a civil manner, but she'd obviously misjudged his character.

"Well, if that is the case, I think you'll need to get a divorce from him, sad though that seems right now," she told Carol.

"Yes, I know that, but I will give him a divorce if that's what he wants as well. I don't want to stay in this marriage if he doesn't want to be with me."

They talked about all this for about an hour, and then Veronica thought it best to leave Carol alone to think things through properly. She felt so sorry, and helpless, faced with such devastating news. When she got home, she burst into tears herself, unable to handle so much grief in one go. Everything seemed to be going wrong suddenly, both her business, which had slowly been declining, and now both her daughters. She thought long and hard about things that night but couldn't think positively about what she might do to help Carol, while Elizabeth was still absent from her life. It became a matter of the deepest concern then in her confused state of mind.

"So much for divinity…" she mumbled to herself then. "If marriage is no longer considered to be divine, what is…?"

Chapter 18

Veronica increasingly blamed herself for Carol's marriage falling apart as the days passed, and she became seriously depressed about it all as it played on her mind. She didn't know what she couldt do to alleviate the situation, and she grew ever more confused. And the more she thought about it, the more depressed she became, in one of those vicious circles it is difficult to escape from, especially when living alone.

She felt a mortifying guilt then about having interfered when Carol had been ill and needed an operation that probably had saved her young life, but she alone had authorised a surgical sterilisation. Perhaps if she hadn't, her daughter's marriage might have turned out to be normal with the natural conception and birth of children. She questioned herself then about if she should be honest about what had taken place and tell Carol the truth about her absence of sterility.

Yet she knew she was incapable of doing this now. Too much time had passed, and Carol was no longer a vulnerable child. She decided then to avoid Carol as much as possible in a bid to lessen her own guilt, even though she knew deep down this would never work. She was the only guilty party, and therefore the present situation was hers to bear alone. But could she do this, seriously? She was already overfilled with doubts, and the shadow of her past troubles followed her around constantly. There was an easy solution, as she well knew, but she really didn't want to go down that road again.

For several days she struggled with all this, like a constant battle for reason and sanity. But then one day while shopping at a local supermarket, she bought three bottles of wine. She placed the wine on the side of her cupboard in the kitchen, where in past times her stock of drink was always displayed and ready.

"Should I have a drink?" she asked herself then several times over the next few hours, trying with all her inner force to resist. "What if that is the only solution to feeling free from all this again...?"

Eventually her resistance broke down, and she poured herself a large glass of wine which she downed with relish. It felt surprisingly good, and she immediately felt a lot better once the alcohol began to take effect. She poured another glass and again downed it in one go, and then another, and that first bottle was quickly emptied. She felt the drink's effect growing on her, but she didn't seem to be overduly worried and opened a second bottle which she soon finished off as well, gaining a false sense of euphoria which she knew wasn't really what she wanted, but how to refrain now started on this downward spiral which she could feel and sense like a light at the end of a long tunnel. Surely, she had the right to some kind of happiness again after so much strife over the long years.

She continued like this for the rest of that evening, at the end of which she was totally drunk and not even thinking about the consequences of what the drink was doing to her, after so long on the wagon and shunning all alcohol.

On an impulse, she then telephoned to Carol, needing to hear a friendly voice.

"Can you come over?" she drawled, sounding completely out of her head, her hands shaking uncontrollably.

Carol couldn't understand a word she was saying, speaking in a slurred voice, and a sudden fear invaded the poor girl's mind.

"Mum, what's the matter? she asked, fearing the worst.

"Nothing's the matter, Carol. I just want to express my love for you, because you've always been my favourite daughter, you know…and I never intended to hurt you in the way that I have, you must believe me…"

"Oh, mum…" Carol shouted, not wanting to believe what she was hearing. "You haven't been drinking, have you?"

"Well, what else could I do, faced with all these problems…"

"Well, don't drink any more, please…I'll come straight over…"

"Thank you…I have something I must tell you…I hope you will be able to forgive me, that's all…"

She hung up, pleased to have spoken to her daughter but still highly upset for not having told her the truth earlier. But she still felt vulnerable and afraid of what Carol's reaction would be on learning the truth, and so she opened the third bottle and drank another full glass of wine. But as she finished the glass, she felt suddenly strange and confused, and as the glass dropped from her hand and smashed on the floor, she passed out and fell heavily to the same floor. She lay there then, still and motionless, looking a total wreck.

When Carol arrived and found her mother lying on the floor in such a pitiable state, she immediately called for an ambulance.

She saw at once that she'd been drinking heavily, the empty wine bottles and smashed glass told her that much. She also realised that she had vomited all over herself and didn't seem to be breathing. She shook her and called her name but got no response. She felt an enormous sense of dread and panic overtake her emotions, knowing but not wanting to know.

When the ambulance arrived, the paramedics hurriedly examined the patient lying motionless on the floor, and after attempting to revive her with oxygen and heart massages, they announced that she was dead and there was nothing more they could do. Carol broke down into tears then, having known but now in shock when the paramedics confirmed her own fears.

"But no...she can't be dead..." she stammered, in shock. "I spoke with her just now before I came over and she sounded okay..."

"Well, I am so sorry, but it seems that she choked on her own vomit. Had she been drinking?"

The empty bottles and the smashed glass were more than was needed for the evident to prevail, and Carol just couldn't take it in that her mother had succumbed again to alcohol after so many years of being sober. What had caused her to crack like that again, with no warning at all? Could it have been her own situation with Mark and the breakup of their marriage? Her mother had seemed very upset on hearing the news, as she now recalled, but why? What secrets had she been harbouring, perhaps, and which now had passed away with her? It was a highly disturbed Carol who perused all those thoughts and questions as her mother's body was wrapped in an impersonal body-bag and taken away to the mortuary at the hospital, where a post-mortem would be undertaken, as is the case for every unexpected death.

Carol left her mother's home and returned to her own empty place, distraught and totally exhausted. Her life seemed to have been a series of dramatic events beyond her control, from her childhood days, and it was difficult for her to come to terms with it all again as she sat and pondered on what had just occurred. Could her mother really have died just like that, without any warning? Or had there been warning signs that she, caught up so much in her own problems, hadn't felt or noticed? Guilt can be like that, a cruel wave of doubt and blame that won't let the victim rest or find peace, no matter how much desired.

"If I'd gone round earlier, I might have been able to save her," she told herself as the guilt kicked in, even though she knew this was untrue.

She sat and thought without relief of any kind, feeling suddenly so terribly alone. Mark was gone. Elizabeth, her sister, had vanished. And now her mother, her rock for so long, had been cruelly taken away in the blinking of an eye, or so it seemed. But why? What had she done to deserve all this? And what could she do now to set her life in motion again, with happiness and fulfilment every day as other people seemed to manage without problems? The dilemma of all bereaved persons, no doubt, but magnified terribly in lonely or isolated people who have no-one to turn to when most they need comfort.

It felt as though another chapter in Carol's life had come to an end, and she knew she would have to find the strength to carry on somehow. She owed that much to her mother, who had loved her, she knew, but who now lay lifeless and alone on a cold mortuary slab.

PART THREE - DESTINY

Chapter 19

The results of the postmortem on Veronica written on the death certificate reported that her death was due to an excessive alcohol intake and a subsequent asphyxiation and choking on vomit. As Carol read the report, she found herself asking if she too wasn't already on the same path as her mother, drinking far too much because of stress and events beyond her control. But she pushed this to the back of her mind as all she could think about right then was her mother's premature death, and whether she was in part to blame for this. The hospital then informed her that they had released her mother's body.

Carol arranged for a local funeral company to collect the body and organise a funeral. She then began planning from her side, visiting a priest at the local Catholic Church to ask that a requiem mass be celebrated for Veronica, as she had been a devout Catholic and she would have wanted such a service. The priest had known Veronica and was sympathetic, and he assured her that Veronica was now with our Lord and at rest from all her torments on this Earth. Following which they fixed a date for the funeral service.

She decided then that she would try to find out as much as she could about Veronica's friends and colleagues and invite them to the funeral. She knew that her mother hadn't mixed a great deal with other people and so it would be a simple service, followed by an interment at the local cemetery. Another stressful point was the fact that she had no way of contacting her sister, Elizabeth, who was still out of touch, but who would surely have attended the funeral were she to know about it. She had always been the most religious one of the family, and it hurt Carol a great deal not being able to contact her. She knew then that she would have to bear it all on her own shoulders, along with Mark, her estranged husband.

She did successfully contact several of the authors who worked with Veronica, as well as some other publishers who agreed to attend the funeral. Veronica's business had become quite successful and known in that milieu, and their presence would be much appreciated in Carol's view.

After the mass and the church service, Carol and Mark stood together at the graveside, accompanied by some of Veronica's local friends and some of the authors who had worked with her while publishing their books. It felt good to have a little support now in this time of sorrow and mourning, and Carol appreciated their presence and condolences. A few even asked her what would happen now to her mother's business, and even though she told them she didn't yet know, it was too soon to think about such things, there was awakened in her thoughts a little worm of an idea that she was unable to shake off. But there were other matters to be taken care of first, as she well knew, and not least her own dismal situation.

She found herself alone then once the service was over. Mark had vanished back to his own new life, wherever that was. The others all dispersed after assuring her of their sympathy, and their willingness to help her if ever she needed help or comfort. That did give her some small comfort already, as the worm of a new beginning slowly took shape at the back of her thoughts.

If only she knew how to contact Elizabeth, she thought again then, as she sat alone in a wake that wasn't a wake, but a cruel and harsh awakening to reality. She was alone. Her mother was gone. Her sister had vanished. And suddenly, the whole world appeared to be a very lonely and hostile place in which she could find no comfort, nor anywhere she might live happily for the remainder of her own life.

She eyed the bottles of wine that still stood in her kitchen, and a wave of disgust swept through her whole body. She knew then that they were the guilty party for both her own and her mother's misfortunes and downfall, and she vowed there and then that never again would she touch a single drop. She had learned the lesson, at least for the time being, and she felt certain that after this tragedy and sorrow she would never again drink, nor allow herself to be led astray or succumb to temptation, as her now absent and sorely missed mother had. The lesson had been absorbed, she felt certain.

Chapter 20

Following several days of deep thought and self-analysis, Carol decided that she must change her lifestyle and move on to different things. She liked the idea of taking over her mother's publishing business and so quit her job at the supermarket. That also solved the problem of being in contact with Mark every day as work colleagues, which would have been unbearable for her.

Mark had visited her again shortly after the funeral, telling her he needed to talk seriously with her about their marriage and their actual situation. It turned out that he had met someone else, as she already suspected, and that this someone was now expecting his child. This really wounded Carol in the face of her own failure and condition, but she remained calm and stoic. It was almost as if she had been expecting this visit and the news he revealed to her.

"We have to initiate a divorce procedure," he added then. "We should act like adults and not hinder each other in the future life we've both decided upon. I hope you can see that and agree?"

"Yes, of course I can," Carol replied, hurt but putting on a brave face. "I know it's my fault we couldn't have children, so I do understand..."

"That's good. I think it's best we remain friends, at least. What are your plans?"

"Well, I've decided to give up my job at the supermarket and take over my mother's publishing business to see if I can make a go of that. She was doing quite well, I think, and it will help me come to terms with her not being here any longer…"

"That sounds like a great idea, really," Mark told her, meaning it. He had loved her and still felt emotionally attached to her.

"Yes, I think so, too…"

"Well, I'm sure you'll make a success of it…and if you need any help or support you can always reach out to me, you know. It's good if we remain friends at least…"

"Yes, all right, thank you…"

"I'll be off now, then. I'll keep in touch and let you know how the divorce is going as it happens…and I really hope you can make a new and happy life for yourself again now…"

"Thank you, Mark…I'll certainly try, whatever happens…"

She felt tears welling up in her eyes as he left, but she knew and accepted that this chapter in her life was now over, and she must move on. She looked at some of the family photos that were scattered around her living room: her mother and father with Elizabeth and herself as children, a happy family group; then her mother alone with the two of them, her father gone forever. That had been the beginning of all changes, as she remembered. And a recent portrait of her mother, smiling and radiant again after living through so much trauma and illness.

Now, she too had vanished, and all she had left were these photos, stark reminders of what had been. Now, she asked herself again, what more was possibly to come? She tried hard to pull herself together again and try to see the future as a better place, unknown, certainly, but surely open to all possibilities. That was her new hope then as she wallowed in her solitude and tried to dream of future happiness.

Chapter 21

Carol then officially took over the running of the publishing company her mother had established. When the will was read out at her solicitor's office, all Veronica's assets, including the business, were to be transferred to Carol, as Elizabeth still couldn't be traced, and so Carol found herself with ample financial resources to carry on with her mother's business, which she knew she had been very proud of.

She met with her mother's employees, and most were quite happy to continue their work with Carol now at the head of the firm. That made things a lot easier, since she had no knowledge of the publishing business nor what it entailed, so working with experienced people would help ease her way into her new role.

She discovered through the established staff that her mother had been planning to publish a monthly magazine, concentrating on fashion and local interest subjects, and she found this project quite attractive. She looked through the files her mother had prepared for this and decided to go ahead with it and try to establish it as a regular source of information and entertainment. As for the title, her mother had left various ideas, but in her own mind she already knew what the title must be: 'Veronica's Dream'. That would be homage enough, she knew.

She recontacted a certain Kimberley, who had worked with her for a while at the supermarket and who, she recalled, had quite some skill in photography. She hoped she would be able to offer some advice on photographic issues and on sales management.

Kimberley agreed at once to join the team, pleased that Carol had thought of her and quite willing to try out her photographic skills in a professional setting.

Next, she advertised for a sales manager, whose task it would be to discover and develop sales outlets for the magazine. Three people applied for the position, whom she interviewed, and from whom she selected a young man named Peter Tierney, who had a good portfolio and seemed the best person for the position. She then began looking for a graphic designer who would design the magazine and its layout, and she contacted an old friend who she knew to be in graphic design. She too agreed to join Carol's team.

Everything was shaping up rapidly, with the magazine's name selected and an enthusiastic staff, and the team began working on the first copy, led by Carol. But once again she started drinking quite a lot in the evenings, finding that alcohol helped her to relax while preparing the magazine for publication and dealing still with the stress of her mother's unexpected death. But mostly she kept a straight head while dealing with the business side of her new life, and the magazine quickly became the focus point of her ambitions.

The sales manager she had taken on, Peter Tierney, was married with two children. He had always believed himself to be happily married until he started work at this new position, where he discovered Carol to be a lovely person and he felt an attraction towards her from the start. But she didn't notice this or show any interest in him in that direction, much to his dismay. As far as she was concerned it was just a business arrangement, and he had to accept this.

He was an intelligent man, and he was always well-dressed and polite. He lived in a semi-detached house with his wife and two children. Originally born in North London, he came from a family consisting of three brothers. He quickly became focused on advancing his career while working for Carol, which he regarded as a wonderful opportunity. Carol initially offered him a two-year contract, and he readily accepted this.

Kimberley was taken on both as photographer and general adviser to Carol, as they knew each other well from having worked together at the supermarket on management levels. Kimberley was now an experienced executive and had been adviser to the supermarket manager during her tenure there. Carol was quite pleased and excited to have her on board.

She had a small daughter named Emily, although she was now separated from her partner, with whom she had never been married. She lived in a small cottage in a rural area, and she was never happier than when sitting in front of a log fire with her daughter, occasionally inviting close friends around for dinner and drinks. Carol had been invited a few times when they were working together at the supermarket, which is how she learned about her photographic skills, although she had never invited many of the staff from the supermarket.

Sarah Austin had become Carol's graphic designer for the new magazine. Sarah had qualified at the age of 26 after studying computers and software in her early twenties at a local college and proved herself exceptionally talented in designing unique projects.

Single and focused on her work, she had found a temporary position at the BBC, working with computers and images. As her contract was coming to an end shortly, she applied for the position of Graphic Designer with Carol's planned magazine. Carol at once thought to herself that it was her gain and their loss and took her on with no hesitation. Together they purchased the computer equipment Sarah would need to be able to work at her best.

When all the staff had been hired and work was ready to begin on the first planned issue, Carol opened a bottle of champagne, and they all toasted their future success. The magazine would be officially launched four weeks hence, and then each month would see a new issue published.

All the employees would work from home, with just Sarah, the graphic designer, working at Carol's house, where she had transformed one of the bedrooms into an office where both she and Sarah could work undisturbed. And so, the work got underway, and Carol felt a deep excitement inside at the thought of continuing her mother's project and dream in this way, as though she was still watching over her and advising her on every aspect of this new project, which was unknown territory still for her. But she would give it her best, she knew. More than that, she couldn't do.

Chapter 22

Carol contacted a model agency with a view to hiring models for the magazine's photo shoots. With Kimberley, they looked through the agency's catalogue of available models and chose three whom they believed would be suitable for their first projects. Kimberley then set up dates and locations for the first test shots. Carol remained in charge of agreeing fees and all invoices and payments that were becoming quite abundant as the project advanced.

Advertisers were also beginning to pay for their rights in the first upcoming issue, so there was a trickle of money already coming in, which was reassuring for all the staff. They all knew that launching a new magazine was at best a risky enterprise, and at worst a surefire way of losing money fast.

Her sales manager, Peter, was becoming increasingly friendly towards Carol, who in turn began to rely upon him quite a lot, especially when she was feeling overwhelmed by it all and sometimes depressed. They went out together now and again for a drink and a chat about the business in the evenings after work, and Carol noticed that this was becoming increasingly frequent. But she thought no more of it than when she went out with other members of her staff, most of whom were soon treated as close friends.

Peter was occupied with visiting businesses on his list of potential advertisers and sponsors, and it was going quite well for him, selling quite a lot of advertising slots. For the first edition he managed to sell eighty spaces in all, and Carol was more than pleased with his efforts. The magazine was shaping up well with the first edition nearing completion. Distribution was then arranged locally and nationally, and within a week or so it would be delivered to all interested outlets.

Carol planned a big celebration for the launch of the magazine, booking a restaurant for a celebratory dinner for all those who had contributed and helped compose the first issue, including the models who appeared in the photo shoots.

But during the evening Carol again seemed to be drinking a great deal of wine, and by the end of the dinner she appeared quite tipsy and had trouble talking steadily with any of the others. Some noticed this, others didn't. But at the end of the evening, Peter saw that she was well out of things and called a taxi to take her home. He then accompanied her to make certain she got home safely and was okay. It was quite late by that time, and he asked Carold if she would mind if he slept in one of her spare bedrooms, as it was too late for him to go home. He had also had a bit too much to drink, if he was honest with himself.

Carol agreed but asked him what his wife might think about such an arrangement. He told her it was nothing for her to worry about, but he just felt too tired now to go home. She staggered drunkenly off to her room, and so he flaked out in one of the spare bedrooms, thinking nothing untoward about the whole situation.

But the following morning, early, he woke with a start and wondered what he was doing there in Carol's house, having spent the night there. After a quick coffee and a reassurance from Carol that nothing had occurred between them, he hurried home, trying to formulate an excuse for his wife about why he'd been out all night, as he hadn't informed her in advance. He told her that he'd been working on the magazine and hadn't noticed the time passing, so had slept there. She seemed to accept this.

Carol had begun drinking wine on a regular basis, and this at times affected her ability to concentrate on her business efforts. Despite this, she managed to continue working. She blamed her drinking on the stress she was feeling while getting the first issue of the magazine ready for publication, and convincing herself that this was just a temporary thing. She still carried the shadow of her mother's past deep inside her: her chronic alcoholism and cure, the neglect of her children, and her eventual death. But none of this could stop Carol from indulging in a glass of wine at each meal, and then often just while relaxing at home in the evenings, prone to melancholic remembrance.

She was more than happy if not a little stressed on receiving the first copies of her new magazine. She leafed through it page by page, and felt happy that it looked so good, like a proper magazine.

"This is for you, mum," she murmured softly, kissing the front cover. "I know you would have been proud of it…"

After work that same day she went with Peter to her local pub, the Crown and Anchor, for a celebratory drink. She was friendly with a lot of the regular customers there and was well-liked, as she was very generous and would always invite some of them to drink with her when she felt lonely.

Peter noticed again just how much she was drinking, and although it worried him, he knew it wasn't his place to tell her that she was drinking too much. Only she could regulate this in herself. He had learned from her in conversations that her mother had once been a chronic alcoholic and had been through a rehabilitation process to cure her. This had set alarm bells ringing in his mind, and he hoped that a similar situation wouldn't occur with Carol.

But if ever he told her that he thought she'd had enough to drink, she would become cagey and aggressive, telling him that she was fine and that he wasn't her keeper. This upset him on several occasions, and he asked himself if the job he had procured with her was as attractive now as he'd first believed it to be.

He took Carol home one day then to meet his wife, Betty, but it was evident from the start that they wouldn't get on very well together. Betty took an immediate disliking to Carol, and when Carol left there was a confrontation between Peter and his wife. She asked him why he was always going out to the pub with that woman, staying out late, and he tried to explain that she was his boss, she paid his wages, and he had to be available for her whenever she needed his advice.

"It's true she sometimes drinks too much," he explained. "And so, I feel I must watch over her and try to keep her out of trouble..."

That appeased his wife a little, but she told him bluntly that she would never trust Carol.

Once the first edition had been distributed and sales were booming, Carol once again invited Peter for a celebratory drink at the pub. She appeared rather subdued and pensive that evening, and Peter was feeling relieved, hoping to get away early for once. But then Carol suddenly perked up and pointed to a man standing alone at the bar.

"I think I know that man," she told Peter. "His face looks very familiar..."

"Where have you seen him before?" Peter asked.

She didn't answer but continued staring hard at the man. just stared at him.

"Would you like another drink?" she asked, obviously an excuse for her to approach the bar. She was puzzled about where she had seen him before, recognising him but unable to pinpoint any details.

She went up to the bar to order another drink and spoke to the man at the bar.

"Excuse me, but don't I know you from somewhere?" she asked.

He turned around and smiled broadly at her

"Hello Carol, don't you recognise me. I was sure it was you when I first saw you sitting over there...""

At first, Carol was surprised. Then a distant recognition and memory flooded through her.

"Is your name Joseph?" she asked in a soft voice.

"Yes," he replied "Don't you remember me? I'm Joseph Fowler, and we used to sit together in the garden at the children's home...."

She was overwhelmed then by a flood of pleasant memories and happiness as she vaguely remembered how close they had been at one time, both alone and deserted by their families and living in the children's home.

"Yes, of course...Joseph Fowler..." she said with a smile. "Gosh, yes, and I think I was a little bit in love with you back then..."

"Really?" he asked with a sly smile.

She realised then that she had loved Joseph Fowler when she was a lonely girl, and she had often wondered what had become of him for some time after they'd been separated and lost touch.

She invited him to join her and Peter at their table.

"Peter, this is Joe, a dear friend of mine from the children's home," she told him.

Surprised, Peter shook Joe's hand, and they sat drinking together a while. But something bothered Peter about this man, and Carol's obvious delight at meeting him again in this way. He couldn't explain it, but there was an air of foreboding about him, while Carol remained oblivious, slightly drunk already and with only eyes for Joe, a shadow from her past.

***

Joseph Fowler was now in his early thirties. After leaving the care home he went to stay with foster parents, a Mr. and Mrs. James, a stable couple who fostered several other children. Joseph got on well with them all, fitting in with the life at the house and soon feeling part of a family; and he always considered Mrs. James to be a mother figure for him.

He left his foster parents at the age of eighteen, legally considered then to be an adult and so independent, and he arranged accommodation with the local council. They expected him to manage his new life independently, but he frequently faced anger issues and had a few minor encounters with law enforcement. Without any parental or established adult guidance, he slowly turned to more serious crime sprees, stealing and shoplifting and suchlike, and being taken to court. He was given warnings and fines, but to no avail, and after one serious robbery he was sentenced to a short prison sentence for theft and fraud. The magistrate told him he hoped this would be a short sharp lesson that would help him get back onto the straight and narrow path of good living.

But of course, it didn't. He met and associated with even more hardened criminals inside the prison, from whom he learned a lot of tricks and ways of earning a crooked living, which he thought to be a good thing for someone like himself, as he could see no bright future ahead.

On being released from prison, he found an apprenticeship through the probation service in which he trained as a plasterer, although he quickly decided that working in a regular job for very low wages wasn't for him, and after a short period of trying to fit in with regular hours and receiving orders, he quit the job and began living on unemployment benefits from the state.

Things then quickly spiralled downwards for him. He stopped paying the rent for his bedsit and was eventually evicted, even though he was receiving housing benefit which covered the cost of his rent. Homeless, he rapidly became dependant on alcohol and mild drugs to stave off the despair of his situation, begging and trying to get money in any way he could, once again stealing from and cheating people he met who tried to help him. It was a hopeless situation, as he well knew, but one from which he seemed incapable to pull himself out of.

Then he happened to bump into Carol that night in the pub, and that set him thinking about how she might be able to help him, and so his hopes were revived beyond all expectations.

She told him briefly about her life since they'd been separated at the children's home, including her mother's sudden death and the launch of a new magazine and the publishing business. As he appeared to be interested, she exchanged phone numbers with him, and they agreed to meet again at the same pub very soon.

Carol felt a huge wave of reminiscence and tenderness flood through her while chatting with Joe, recalling how he'd been the only one with whom she'd had a real contact with during that difficult period, and even though they'd been little more than children at the time, she realised now that a love had developed between them, which had then been interrupted by circumstance. But now it appeared to have returned, almost like a fateful step both had possibly been seeking without knowing it.

Of course, Joe said very little about his own life, the numerous hardships he'd faced and was still struggling with. He immediately saw her as a possible lifebelt and so kept quiet about his own problems. He'd become a dab-hand at inventing stories about himself, and Carol was taken in as most other interlocutors were. If she had known then what challenges lay ahead, she most probably would never have contacted him again.

Chapter 23

Carol's magazine "Veronica's Dream" ran through a lot of successful editions as it became known and more popular, thanks mostly to the diligent work of the staff she had taken on. But her constant drinking and reliance on alcohol started to cause significant problems, as she left most of the important decisions concerning the magazine to the staff who were now running it. Peter remained a firm support, but this led to conflicts with his wife, who repeatedly asked him to stop seeing her. But he ignored her requests, telling her once again that this was the best job he'd ever found and denying any suggestion that he had other motivations.

And yet Carol and Peter were going more frequently for a drink after working together all day, and this wasn't looking good for those around them. The other staff members began to comment, and tensions were growing. Both Carol and Peter ignored all this, though, while enjoying each other's company.

Then Carol suggested one evening that he take a holiday with his family in Spain, staying at the apartment her father had bequeathed to her many years before and which she hardly used, now she was so busy with the business. He thought this very generous of her and accepted graciously. It also pleased his wife, who saw another side to Carol then, even if it was calculated rather than spontaneous. She thought it would be good for Peter and herself to be away from her for a couple of weeks.

Peter enjoyed his holiday with his family, although he found himself missing Carol a lot. He knew that he'd rather be alone with her in Spain than with his wife and children. He tried to hide his feelings but found the going difficult at times.

After a week, he telephoned to Carol and noticed right away that she sounded intoxicated, her voice slurred.

"No, no, I'm fine," she told him when he commented on this. "Are you enjoying your holiday?"

"Yes, very much" he replied. "But I'm missing you an awful lot, you know..."

"That's good," she said with a giggle. "I mean, that you're all enjoying yourselves. But I must tell you that I'm now with Joe...you remember him, the man we met at the pub, and who was in the home with me when we were kids?"

"Ah, yes, him..." Peter replied, recalling his first impressions of that man. He wasn't too pleased on hearing that she had taken up with him again. "What do you mean, you're now with him?"

"Well, to be honest, I think I still love Joseph, and I really want to be with him again, and so that's what I'm doing at the moment..."

"Well, I just hope you know what you're doing, Carol. And I'll see you when I get back..."

Peter's holiday didn't evolve quite so well after receiving this distressing news from Carol. Despite being with his wife and children, he was fully aware of his own feelings towards Carol, who now appeared to be rejecting him for this shady drifter named Joe. He also feared for the future of the magazine and his own employment with it, having understood how fickle Carol could be, and how she was leaning ever more upon the strength her drinking seemed to give to her. A false courage, as he well knew. Indeed, as Carol also knew when she recalled her mother's own walk down that road of ruin and death.

He was keen then to get back home and speak with her face to face, to find out precisely what was happening and what had occurred during his absence. He feared the worst. He felt that this Joe character wasn't at all trustworthy and more than likely to exploit her in her feeble state of mind. And that thought did worry him a lot.

***

Meanwhile, Carol found herself struggling with her deteriorating mental health, brought on by over-drinking and perhaps too much responsibility with the business she had taken over from her mother. Confusion over her feelings for both Peter and Joe only added to the sense of unbalance she was feeling increasingly often now, and she decided then one morning to consult a doctor about all this.

The doctor had checked her medical history and discovered that there had been incidents in the past when she'd suffered bouts of anxiety and depression, as well as the physical problems she'd gone through whilst a young teenager in care, and he suggested she went for a consultation at the local Mental Health Hospital. She thanked the doctor and felt almost a wave of relief, knowing she had to do something to pull herself together again. When she returned home, she worked a little on the magazine in progress and didn't drink at all that evening.

She quickly received an appointment to talk with a psychiatrist at the hospital. During the consultation, he questioned her about her life and work and the difficulties she was now experiencing in her everyday life. He also asked about her drinking habits, and other things that were affecting her lately. She was honest with him and admitted she was drinking far too much, just as her mother had, and she was worried about this affecting her life and her work.

He listened and made notes, then he told her that they could help her, but it would mean her temporary admission to the hospital as a volunteer inpatient. Carol felt relieved that she was now going to get some professional help with her mental health issues and thanked the doctor.

"Are you willing to come into the hospital as a voluntary patient, then?" the doctor asked.

"Yes, I am," she told him. "But what sort of timeline would I be looking at?"

"That depends a lot on your progress, but I should say roughly about two weeks. Once we treat you with the proper medication, improvements may occur sooner, of course. And again, the sooner you check in, the sooner you'll be able to leave and carry on with your normal life…"

"All right, I'll bear that in mind. I could check in as soon as tomorrow even, if I can get things organised today…"

"That would be good. I look forward to seeing you again very soon then."

On leaving the hospital she returned home to find Peter and some of the other staff working on the forthcoming issue of the magazine. She spoke to Peter about what she had decided.

"I'll be hospitalised for about two weeks and was wondering if you could manage everything while I'm away, and carry on with getting the new magazine ready? I do understand this is a big demand on my part, but it would help if you could."

"Of course, I'd be more than happy to help out. It's nothing too serious, I hope?"

"Not really, I just need some rest and some help to get over a few issues..."

"Does Joseph know about this?"

"Yes, of course, I've let him know but he's away on business at the moment. I'll wait and see if he comes to visit me."

"I understand.... you can count on me, anyway, and I'll keep things running smoothly..."

"Thank you, Peter...I'm happy you're still standing by me after all that has happened lately..."

She felt somewhat guilty without really knowing why. She knew that Peter was very fond of her, and that the reappearance of Joseph in her life had hurt him a little, but she told herself that he was still happily married and that she had no right to disturb him in his life.

Joseph was another kettle of fish completely, and she now harboured a lot more doubts and worries on his behalf. He often disappeared for several days at a time and couldn't be contacted, and this was another worry for her. He always told her that he'd been away on 'business' but would never elaborate. She even asked herself if he wasn't in some unconscious way partly responsible for her present state of mental health and worries, although she wouldn't admit to this. The bond between them stretched far back, and it seemed like a coup of providence had brought them together again. She hoped it was, anyway. The rest was her destiny, she felt sure, and she had no control over that any longer.

Chapter 24

Carol checked herself into the mental hospital the very next day, anxious to get her life back on track as soon as she could. She was escorted to a private room, which pleased her, as she wouldn't have enjoyed having to share a room with other patients, or worse, being placed on a general ward.

One of the nurses helped her to settle in and then proceeded through the usual new patient's routine of checking blood pressure and other possible ailments, taking a blood sample which her doctor would need to detect anything out of the ordinary that could be affecting her mental health. She felt relaxed and relieved almost immediately, as though the world and all its problems had been lifted from her shoulders and that now she might recover her sense of happiness and contentment, something she'd long felt missing.

The nurse then accompanied her on a short tour of the hospital, explaining where to find the dining room and other amenities she might enjoy during her stay. Carol explained that she was only there for a short stay and hoped to be leaving within a couple of weeks. The nurse smiled and said she understood. So many patients said the same thing, whereas many ended up living there on a permanent basis. But she felt that Carol was serious and wished her all the best. The treating doctor would see her the following day.

The next day, Carol was called to see her treating psychiatrist for a one-to-one consultation about the treatment he thought she should receive. She felt pleased that he had called her and seemed to take an interest in her problems. He thanked her for coming and reassured her that everything she shared would remain confidential. That also made her feel more at ease.

"So, can you please tell me in your own words what you think has led you to this crisis in your life? That way I can determine what may have contributed to your current situation and brought you here to seek some help..."

She told him then about her childhood, and the trauma that being placed into a Catholic children's home run by nuns had caused her, even though it was only for a short period. Her mother had become a chronic alcoholic after the death of her husband — Carol's father — and had spent months in a rehabilitation centre.

"So, you didn't enjoy that stay in the children's home?"

"No, not at all, I really hated it, I think. It was run by the nuns, and my younger sister, Elizabeth, fell under their influence and eventually became a nun herself when she was older. Since then, she's gone missing and hasn't been in touch with us for a very long time. It broke my mother's heart, I think, and Elizabeth didn't even attend the funeral, although I tried everything I could to find her and let her know what had happened. I found out that she had left the convent and married a man she had met there, but I still don't know where she is, and I think that has also contributed to my own state of depression and anxiety."

"Yes, I can understand that," the doctor told her. "But I see that you were married as well for a time, and that your own marriage ended, yes?"

"Yes, sadly. My husband really wanted to start a family, but then we found out that I couldn't conceive, and I still don't know why. Anyway, he met someone else and is now married to her and has a child, so he probably made the right decision. My mother knew all about this, and I think she knew about my infertility, although she would never discuss it with me, as though she was afraid of the truth..."

"I see. I have studied your medical records, of course, and I saw that when you were aged fourteen you underwent some serious surgery for digestion and stomach troubles you'd been suffering with. Do you remember any of that?"

"Yes, I do, vaguely. I had some disease that upset my digestion, I think, and I stopped eating for a while. That's when my mother agreed for me to have an operation to cure it, which I think it did, but it's all a bit hazy now. But sometimes I do think about all that and wonder if everything that happened to me was my fault or my mother's, because she hadn't looked after me and my sister properly because of her drinking too much...and sometimes all that makes me cry myself to sleep..."

"Well, that's understandable, Carol. Your actual state of depression has certainly been brought about by what has happened to you recently, as well as your troubled childhood still lurking in the shadows. But I think we can treat you for this, with some mild medication and a little one to one therapy with one of our therapists. Then hopefully you'll be able to carry on running your business and live a stable and normal life in the future..."

"Thank you, doctor. It would be good if I could chase out all those past shadows and look to the future again, and stop drinking, of course. I think that has a lot to do with it all and recalling what my mother went through for the same reasons."

"Yes, I agree, and that is one of the prerequisites for a successful outcome. Alcohol also counteracts against the medication you'll be prescribed, so it is important that you find the willpower to resist..."

"I do understand that," Carol told him, feeling a little ashamed.

"All right then, I'm going to prescribe some mild antidepressants which I think will help raise your spirits. And I'd like you to remain here as a patient for around a week or so, and then we can get you sorted out with the therapy and other things and hopefully get you back home and back to work again. Is that acceptable for you?"

"Yes, that sounds fine. Thank you, doctor..."

She left the doctor's office with the feeling that her well-being was now being considered and looked after, and she already felt a lot better inside. The nurse came to see her shortly after and helped her take her first tablet for antidepression. It seemed simple to her then, and she wondered why things always appeared to be so complicated inside her own thoughts. She was confident then that in a week's time she would be back home and running the magazine and the rest of her business with a clear head.

A couple of days later a nurse came into Carol's room and told her that she had a visitor, who was waiting for her in the day room. She saw Joseph Fowler smiling at her as soon as she entered the near-empty room, and her heart raced a little. He had come back then, and more, he had come to see her at the hospital, which meant that he had received her messages. She approached him and put her arms around him, greeting him with a warm kiss.

"I have missed you, Joe," she murmured softly.

"And I've missed you, too, Carol. But tell me, when are you leaving this place?"

"In about a week or so, if all goes well," she told him.

"But what's wrong with you," he asked, a look of concern on his face. "I mean, why did they put you here, in a mental hospital?"

"Well, I volunteered to come here to be honest," she explained calmly. "I've been feeling a bit depressed lately and I was drinking far too much because of that and trying to get over it. Things just seemed to be getting on top of me, and I was thinking about my poor mother and what she went through and how she ended up and I really don't want to go down that same path, you understand?"

"Yes, of course I do, and I'm sorry I wasn't around when you probably needed me to be. But rest assured, Carol, I'm here now to support you and help you in any way I can."

"Thank you, that's good to know…"

She asked him then about what he'd been doing when he was away from her, and he explained that he'd been trying to make a living for himself again, but it was difficult without having any transport. If he could find some regular work again, then they could have some really good times together again.

"But if you'd told me all this when we met up again, I could have helped you, really. You know I'm running my own business now, the one my mother built up, and I'm sure you could work with us somehow if that's what you wanted..."

"Thanks, Carol, but you know, I really need to stand on my own two feet and pull myself up from the depths again. I don't want you to think I'm interested in you just to help me, really, so that's why I need to find myself a good job and earn my own money and then we can consider other things together, I hope..."

Carol looked hard into his eyes, and she believed everything he was saying, he seemed so sincere. It made her recall the time they were youngsters together in the children's home, and how when they had spoken together and told each other secrets and made plans to be together in the future. That pleased her a lot, and it seemed that a circle had been completed, as though they were meant to be together from their very first meeting.

"Have you got anything lined up at all now?" she asked him then.

"I've got a good contact in the building trade who's constructing a few new houses, and he's offered me a job as a plasterer if I want it. The problem is that I need to find a car or a van so that I can commute every day, as it's quite a way out and buses are no good for that kind of regular work..."

"Well, why don't you borrow my car for a while, since I hardly ever use it these days?"

"That would be great, really. But are you sure?"

"Yes, why not? And that would be a good excuse for me to see you again more often as well…." she laughed.

"That is kind of you, and it would certainly make it much easier for me to get to work every day."

"Well, that's decided, then. It's parked outside my house, and I'll give you the keys when you leave, then you can take it and use it as you need. And if anyone is at the house working, as they are most days, you can explain things to them. Peter knows who you are anyway…"

"Thank you, Carol. That will be a huge help for me right now…"

Carol was so enraptured with Joe again that she couldn't even imagine that he might be lying to her about his life and intentions. He hadn't worked at a proper job since he'd left school, and in truth he didn't want to work. His stints in prison and mixing with other villains had set him on a path he was unable to leave, and so she believed him when he told her that he was an experienced plasterer with a lot of jobs just waiting for him, and all with excellent salaries. He went on to tell her that he could also help her around the house with any decorating she might need and take care of her garden. Naively, she believed everything he told her.

"I was thinking of converting my loft into a spare bedroom, actually" she told him then with a smile. "Perhaps you could help me with that?"

"Of course I will," he replied." It could be a special place then for just the two of us, like we used to imagine back at that kid's home..."

She liked that idea immensely, and his smiling eyes told her that he meant it. It felt as though their childish dreams of a future together were about to be realised, and she felt a hundred times better already by simply spending an hour with him and talking as they'd always talked, secretly and passionately, while still children at the home.

Carol asked him then if he'd like to go for a coffee at the restaurant in the hospital, and he said he would. He then told her he hadn't eaten anything since the day before, a lack of time and the worry about her had made him forget even to eat, and so they went to the public restaurant together. Again, she was completely taken in by his concern for her. He had evolved into a talented actor over the years, and now this served him well.

She ordered a complete breakfast for him, which he wolfed down hungrily, causing her to smile a little. She had just a coffee. She had the bill added to her hospital account, and then he accompanied her back to her room, as his visit was ended and she had therapy appointments to attend. She looked for her car keys and handed them to him. He smiled warmly and thanked her.

"I'll think of you every time I'm driving," he told her. "Then we'll soon be together again..."

"But have you got a place to stay right now?" she asked, concerned again.

"Well, I've been dossing around on a few mates' settees to be honest," he admitted, looking like a naughty schoolboy who'd been caught while up to some mischief.

"So why don't you just stay at my place for the time being?" she suggested. "You'd have the place to yourself until I'm back home, and Peter and the others won't mind if I call and tell them you'll be there in the evenings."

"That would be fantastic!" he replied with a broad grin. "But are you sure? I mean, I don't want to impose upon you right now with all your own problems to sort out..."

"Don't worry, Joe, I'll be fine. And when I do come home, we'll sort something else out for you if you want, so it won't be a bother. And you've got my loft to convert as well, don't forget!"

"Well, thank you, Carol. You really are being good to me, and I'll make it up to you when you're home again, I promise. It does seem like we're fated to be together again, somehow..."

"And that's exactly what I'm feeling right now, Joe..."

They shared a passionate kiss, and then she handed him her house keys with a warm smile.

"Hurry up and get well," he told her then. "I'll be waiting for you..."

"I will," she replied, feeling a new motivation deep inside to get well and to be back home with this man who appeared so warm and loving, and with whom she had shared secrets in the past that only they knew of.

He hurried away then, carrying the keys to her car and house and feeling quite smug and pleased with himself. Things had worked out for him far better than any plans he might have harboured before their meeting, and he hurried away to see what was waiting for him at her home. All thoughts of Carol had suddenly disappeared as he diverted his attention towards his own plans for the future, seemingly unaffected by the great passion she had demonstrated towards him. As with the enormous help she had handed meekly over to him on a plate.

Chapter 25

A week later, Carol was discharged from the hospital after the doctor had confirmed that she should be fine while taking her medication. She telephoned to Joe to ask him to pick her up from the hospital, but she got no reply. She presumed he was busy at work somewhere. She decided then to give Peter a call, who was more than happy to pick her up. She was waiting for him in the entrance, and he was pleased to see her smiling and looking so well. He hugged her warmly and kissed her on the cheek. She looked and felt radiant.

While driving to her house, he asked her why Joe hadn't come to pick her up. She explained that she had called him but couldn't get an answer, as he was probably working away somewhere.

Peter didn't like Joe. He knew instinctively that he wasn't good news for Carol, and he couldn't understand why she'd become involved with him again. She'd told him about their distant past, how he had been her only friend while growing up in the children's home, and it was obvious to him that Joe was playing now on that history together. But he felt unable to interfere or do anything about it. He still loved Carol dearly himself, and was sorely disappointed that she was now in a relationship with Joe, despite himself being married.

When they arrived at the house, they saw that her car was parked on the drive. She found that odd, having believed Joe to be absent at work. They went in together and found Joe in the kitchen drinking a coffee. Carol went straight to him and held him in her arms in a warm hug. She felt happy then to be home.

"I didn't know you were coming home today," he explained vaguely.

"Well, I tried calling you, Joe, but got no answer, so that's when I called Peter…"

"Oh, I'm so sorry," he stuttered. "I was charging my phone and probably didn't hear it…"

She accepted his explanation without suspicion. Peter simply stood there looking on, thinking once again how this man, Joe, was using her for his own ends and wishing he was somewhere else. When Carol asked him if he'd like a coffee, he made an excuse, telling her that he had some work to complete for another company he'd started working with part-time as a sales representative. He was selling new cars for a local Toyota dealer. Inside, he found it difficult to accept that Carol had become so deeply involved with this man, whom he didn't trust.

When Peter left the house, Joe took Carol's hand and pulled her close to him, kissing her with passion and whispering to her that he loved her. Carol returned his kiss, surprised as she was by such an unexpected outburst.

"I do care about you, Joe, and I want us to stay together now..."

He unbuttoned her blouse very slowly, kissing her gently all the while and whispering sweet nothings into her ear.

"Oh, Carol, your perfume is driving me crazy, and I really want to be with you as well now…"

Suddenly out of control herself, she unbuttoned his shirt and her hands roamed all over his muscular chest, while he responded in kind, gently caressing her warm breasts. He undid the side of her skirt, and it dropped to the floor as she unbuttoned his trousers and belt. He picked her up then and headed towards her bedroom.

For an instant their combined mad passion and lust filled them both with ecstasy, until their senses were finally calmed and satisfied, and they lay in each other's arms, talking softly and making vague plans for a future life to be spent together. Carol felt so happy again and wondered why she had been obliged to spend time in a psychiatric hospital when all she really needed was to love and be loved, as she felt was the case there now, lying in her bed in Joe's strong and comforting arms. With such thoughts running through her head she fell into a deep sleep, with Joe lying beside her, a huge grin written across his own face, as though celebrating a victory of his own.

Chapter 26

Peter, meanwhile, was obliged to accept that his brief attraction to and infatuation with Carol was now over. With Joe back on the scene, there was no way he could let himself become involved with her, and even though it was painful, he had to face the reality of his situation and get on with his own life. His marriage was on the rocks as well now, as he knew, because of his prior involvement with Carol, even though it had never gone very far, and certainly not as far as he would have liked. His wife was hyper-jealous, however, and wouldn't stand any other woman setting her sights on her husband. That had been Peter's biggest mistake. Now, she told him that she wanted a divorce from him, the sooner the better, and then he could carry on with his fancy boss-lady as much as he wanted.

His protests fell upon deaf ears. Their years of being together and raising children held no sway with her now. But he must leave them as soon as was possible and try to make his own way in the future. He knew that she wouldn't be talked around and reluctantly accepted his fate. What else could a man do?

At the same time, he felt that he could no longer work with Carol, even though he had enjoyed working for and with her over the past few months, building up her magazine business as best he could while earning a comfortable living. In an ideal world, he might well have ended up living with her, a couple in love and running a successful business together, as in his distant dreams. Now all that was erased from his mind, and he had to tell her that he was quitting the job and making new plans for his future. He couldn't abide seeing her with Joe when he worked from her office at her home, knowing that he meant little to her now apart being an employee.

He called on Carol one morning when he saw that her car was absent, which meant that Joe was probably out with it. She was pleased to see him, as usual, and believed he'd come to work on the next issue of the magazine with her. She was much surprised when he informed her solemnly that he had to quit the job and had come to let her know.

"What has happened, Peter? I mean, I thought you loved your job with me and the magazine…"

"I do, it's not the job that's the problem, but my own situation now. My wife wants a divorce, mostly because she's jealous of all the time we've spent together alone here at your house and going out together for drinks, and now you've become involved with that Joe, well, it just seems unfair on all of us to carry on as we have been. As I told you, it's not the job at all, I have enjoyed working with you and helping make the magazine a success for you. But now I have this other job with the garage, selling cars and all that, and it just seems to be more up my street right now."

"Well, this is a shock for me, Peter. I really didn't mean to upset your wife in any way at all, it's just that we became friends as well as working together, and after all my problems it was just nice to have you close and helping me when I was down. I hope you can understand that?"

"Yes, of course, I'm not blaming you for anything, it's all my fault, I know, and so the best thing is for me to disappear so you can get on with your life with Joe, and I'll remake my own life somewhere else while doing the job I enjoy most, selling cars…"

"Well, I do appreciate everything you've done for me, Peter, really, I do. Without your help I would never have got the magazine off the ground, and you've helped make it successful as much as anyone else has…"

"And I appreciate all you've done for me, Carol. My personal affairs are nothing to do with you or the work we've done together, so you shouldn't think that. I know you've had serious problems, and I just hope that now you'll be able to get on with your life and be happy again…there's no reason why you shouldn't be."

"Thank you, Peter. I will never forget you, whatever, you can be sure about that."

They separated on good terms, both saddened but knowing it was for the best. He left immediately, having brought all his work documents with him for her to continue with his side of the business, and she wrote him a very generous bonus cheque to show how much she'd appreciated all he'd done for her over the past months. And that was the end of their relationships, social and workwise.

Chapter 27

When Joe returned home, Carol told him what had occurred with Peter, how he'd left her somewhat in the lurch and that she would have to find a new sales manager quickly to keep the magazine going.

"And what does that work entail?" Joe asked, suddenly seeming curious.

"Well, a sales manager handles sales and distribution of the magazine, as well as looking for new clients to advertise with us, and chasing up existing advertisers to renew their contracts and all that…"

"You know, I think I might be able to handle that for you…"

"Really?" Carol asked, surprised.

"Why not? I think I have pretty good communicative skills from the many jobs I've already done, and it would help us be together a lot more as well, like keeping it all in the family…"

Carol was surprised at this offer and wasn't sure if he was serious about it. She'd never thought of Joe in such a way, knowing him to be a man used to working with his hands rather than his head. She doubted if he'd be up to the task of sales manager, with the work and constant travel involved. But then she thought it might be worth giving him a chance to prove himself, and it would certainly mean that she'd get to see a lot more of him.

"Okay," she told him. "Let's give it a try, shall we? You can always change your mind if you feel it's not your kind of work, so it won't matter. And as you said, it would mean spending a lot more time with each other, as a lot of the work has to be done online here in the office, as well as actual travel and canvassing. What do you think?"

"I'm up for it, don't you worry. And I can start right away, as my other job has just come to an end..."

"Well, that is handy," Carol smiled, still not suspecting anything untoward. "But we'll have to get you a smart new suit and everything, so you look the part when visiting potential clients..."

"Of course," Joe agreed, smiling back. "But at the moment I don't have any ready money available, until I get paid for the job I've just finished..."

"Well, I can advance you the money, no problem, and I'll soon be paying you a salary as well, so we can work it all out from that later on...would £600 be enough, do you think?"

"Yes, that would be fine," he said. "If you deposit the money into my account I can buy a new suit, some shirts, and a couple of smart ties..."

"Okay, I'll do that, and then I can come with you and help choose some smart clothes if you like..."

Joe looked a little put out by this offer, although Carol hardly noticed, so pleased was she that they would be working and living together from then on.

"Oh, I'd rather go alone, if you don't mind," he told her, covering his unease as best he could. "I don't like shopping much anyway and it'll be a lot quicker on my own. Then I can surprise you with my new look when I get back. Do you mind?"

"No, I understand, so don't worry. I've got such a lot to do now anyway, getting things in order and chasing up the other staff to see how the new issue is coming along. I'll see you later when you get back..."

She transferred the £600 into his bank account and he went off on his shopping spree feeling quite light-headed. He liked the idea of having money again, and he felt that now this would become a regular thing with Carol's backing. He was already formulating plans for his future, of which she was to be one of the principal elements.

He visited a local charity shop that sold second-hand clothes at very low prices and managed to find a dark grey suit that looked new, plus a few shirts and ties that would fit the part he had to play. The whole purchase was under £50, and so the remainder of Carol's money was his to do with as he wished. Pleased with his own cunning, he spent some time then drinking with old friends and associates in a pub, formulating other plans that had no bearing at all on Carol's plans for him. What she didn't know wouldn't hurt her, and that was his reasoning at the time.

His deception towards Carol continued then when he was supposed to begin working as her sales manager, driving around in her car seeking out new clients for advertising in the magazine. He told her that he'd visited a lot of different companies who were very interested, and which would contact her in the near future to set things up. She listened to him with a smile, again believing everything he told her while supplying him with a constant stream of cash to cover his travelling expenses. She had no reason to suspect anything untoward at that time.

In truth, he was spending most of his time at different pubs and clubs with his gang of old friends, most of whom were villains and layabouts. He appeared to them to be always flush with money and generous with buying them drinks, and so they encouraged him, of course, most seeing him as an easy touch. Meanwhile, Carol was at home, still believing that he was out representing and acquiring customers for advertising and distributing her magazine.

She busied herself putting the next issue of the magazine together while keeping the financial side of the business in hand, checking invoices and making sure the next issue was covered financially. She was counting a lot on the business Joe was supposedly building up with new advertisers, but when nothing new arrived in the office she began to worry a little, wondering what was going on and why none of the supposed advertisers had actually contacted her with firm orders.

He'd be out all day with her car, coming back to the house in the evening to tell her that he hadn't had much success that day but he'd try again the following day, as he still had many contacts to try, and again she fell in with his stories, wanting desperately to believe that he really was trying and so she should give him a chance to prove himself. She did harbour a few nagging doubts after a while, however, but she pushed them to the back of her mind. She refused to become depressed again.

One evening he returned later than usual, and Carol could see that he'd been drinking, but she said nothing. Then he asked her if she'd like to go out with him for dinner at one of their favourite restaurants, and she gladly agreed. She thought it would do them good to get out of the house and hopefully clear the air about his lack of success in his new job.

Looking pleased with himself, he opened a bottle of wine and poured out two glasses and offered one to Carol, even though she'd vowed not to drink again after her recent stay at the mental hospital. But he insisted, just one glass to celebrate, and she ceded to his pressure. She did find it comforting, although she knew she shouldn't. Then they set off together to the restaurant, with Joe driving her car.

During the meal, Joe talked about Carol's business affairs and the magazine, hinting that he wasn't really suited for the job of sales manager without actually stating this openly. He then went on to ask why she'd remained in touch with her ex-husband, who, he noticed, had been round to the house a few times doing odd jobs of maintenance and redecoration at Carol's request, work for which she paid him. He suggested then that she used him instead for such work, as he was experienced in building and far better suited for that than what he was attempting to achieve for her as sales manager. She looked at him in surprise, as he'd been so enthusiastic at the start of their work together.

At one point he disappeared to the gents' toilets, leaving her to ruminate over all this, wondering a little if she'd once again made a bad choice by becoming involved with Joe again, knowing so little really about his past. He was gone rather a long time, and when he returned, she noticed white smudges across his nose and chin, which he quickly rubbed off when she asked about them.

"It's like a talc they have in there to refresh people," he explained in a rushed voice, although she knew better, even if she pushed her suspicions aside.

Carol felt rather taken aback by all this, especially as he kept refilling her glass with wine and insisting that she drink with him, as to drink alone wasn't a good thing in his view. He continued in this line of conversation throughout the meal, and Carol felt quite befuddled when they eventually left the restaurant to return home together. Carol, of course, paid the bill, which was quite hefty after the many bottles of wine they'd got through.

Once home, Joe continued talking about redesigning her house for her, dazzling her with suggestions and ideas which she lapped up hungrily. She felt quite intoxicated both with the wine and his talk about work and love and their togetherness, failing to see that he was in fact digging his own way further into her life and her finances. He was very adept at talking people into giving him what he wanted from them, and by the time they went to bed he had managed to persuade her that he would turn her house into a palace where she would be his queen. Contented, she fell asleep in his arms, not seeing his wicked smile of success as he planned ever further ahead.

Chapter 28

Carol was convinced that she loved Joe and that he was in love with her, and she believed that he would always be honest with her and their business arrangements. She was in for a bit of a shock when she eventually discovered the truth about him, but that was still far ahead in the future.

In truth, he had already formulated a plan uniquely for his own benefit, and he used her gullibility to discover as much as he could about her own financial situation and the many assets she owned. Whenever she was out alone or occupied in her office with the business, he dug and delved as much as he could, learning that apart from the business left to her by her mother, she also owned her late mother's house, left to her and her sister, plus an apartment in Spain, left to her by her father. He even managed to access her bank accounts and was pleased to find her well provided for, which in his mind represented a fortune. He felt he was in the right place then and worked on staying there and getting what he could from the situation.

Carol suspected none of this, so happy she felt in his constant company now. Ignoring his apparent idleness, which he told her was due to past illnesses and mental fatigue, she supported him in every way she could. This suited him absolutely. He would spend all morning in bed while she was busy working, and then he would demand that she cook his meals and generally take care of him, all the while fussing around in a loving fashion to make her feel wanted and cared for.

He was still using her car as though it now belonged to him, and she relied on him to drive her when she needed to go somewhere for the business, or even on shopping trips.

"You've got your own unpaid chauffeur now!" he would laugh, and she joined in his amusement as one of their private jokes.

"Well, I'm really happy about that," she told him. "And for all the other things you do for me…"

"My pleasure," he smiled back, pleased with himself and his own cunning.

The promised remodelling and decoration of her home also stagnated once he'd incrusted himself into her life, and he always came up with some excuse about why it wasn't advancing any faster. He was really exhausted, he needed more time, a friend who'd promised to help had let him down, and so forth. She accepted his explanations with an understanding smile, hoping he would soon recover and get back to his former lively self.

Then he'd ask her to pay the bill for his mobile phone, which seemed extraordinarily high to her, but he again explained it away by telling her he was making a lot of calls abroad for a new business venture that would soon bring in a great deal of money. Again, she believed him, so sincere did he appear to be at such moments.

He often went out alone in the evenings, returning in the early hours of the morning when she would be in bed, although she was always awake when he did come back, staggeringly drunk as a rule and making a lot of noise, cursing and swearing incoherently and causing her to recall similar nights with her ex-husband.

She also remembered how that had ended, blaming herself, of course. Was she destined then to relive the same pattern of events over and over throughout her life, as though under a curse she was unable to shake off? She never once thought about blaming Joe for what was happening, because she felt her love for him was above all that. Joe relished it all quite happily when he was sober, playing along with her in his own calculated saga of greed and deception.

She remained convinced that she did love him and that he loved her, and she couldn't imagine her life now without his constant presence, even when he was ever more absent. When they did go out together in the evenings, very rarely now, he always drank far too much and encouraged her to do so as well, and they would end up arguing about trivial matters which annoyed him a lot, and he often stormed away and left her alone to settle the bill and take a taxi home, alone and in tears. But she still couldn't see through his blatant lies and strategy, blinded by her own intense feelings towards him, as though he might be a wayward son, the one she could never conceive and rear as her own.

She was also drinking increasingly again, despite her fears and bitter memories, as it seemed to ease the stress of each day and made her feel more able to cope with his erratic behaviour, which seemed to be worsening by the day. She realised that he was also using a lot of drugs as well as drinking far too much, although she refrained from saying anything as she knew this would only enrage him and more arguments would follow. She craved the calm of their first days together and naively believed that things would get better over time.

But of course, they didn't. On the contrary, she soon discovered that Joe was also clandestinely dealing drugs, supplying to people he met during his evenings out with friends, although again she was too afraid to confront him about this. Then, while tidying his wardrobe one morning, she came across a shoe box filled with dozens of sachets containing a white powder. She knew at once what it was.

There were also a few thick wads of banknotes, which only confirmed her suspicions. So, all his pleading of poverty and demands for help were another part of his strategy, although she still found it hard to believe and accept. She feared his temper and arguments now, and so kept quiet, hoping things would calm down again eventually.

Things came to a head one night after he had staggered noisily into the kitchen after a night out with his friends. Carol felt seriously annoyed again and got out of bed, determined to confront him for once. Enough was enough.

She found him crouching over the kitchen table, sniffing cocaine through a rolled-up banknote. Struck speechless for a while, she looked on in horror. He was actually using drugs in her home, and she realised at once all the possible repercussions. How could he possibly do such a thing?

"Joe!" she cried eventually, startling him a little. "What are you doing in my kitchen?"

"Ah, Carol, my sweetheart, is that you?" he answered in a drunken slur. "Why don't you come and join me, eh...you'll really love the effects, I'm sure...much better than drinking..."

Carol was horrified at the thought, and wanted to run away, to be rid of this man who was no longer the Joe she had known as a child and whom she had fallen in love with, against all common sense, as she now realised. But she stayed where she was, watching, a little fascinated, while trying to come to terms with something that was far too overwhelming now for her confused state of mind. Which he well knew about, of course.

"Come on, don't be afraid, one little sniff won't hurt you, and you'll be amazed afterwards when we go to bed and make love how fantastic you'll feel, like never before, believe me...real extasy..."

She gave in then, partly persuaded by his words and his sincere look of devotion towards her and partly wanting everything to be ecstatic again between them. She sat beside him at the table as he prepared the cocaine in two strips for both of them to share. He explained what to do, then demonstrated by sniffing the first strip deeply and violently into his nostril. She watched, fascinated, as his reaction echoed around the kitchen with roars and splutterings he couldn't control. Was it really that good, and safe? She hesitated a moment, but he was already alert again and on to her, aiding her as best he could.

She followed his lead, snorting delicately the trail of cocaine with his encouragement, and after a few seconds she didn't know what had hit her as her senses reeled and her whole being seemed lifted into the air somehow, almost like flying. His beaming face was close to hers, and he kissed her passionately as she tried to contain and understand what was happening to her, but all resistance was useless, as she now found out.

He prepared two more lines of the drug, which they snorted in turn, and Carol found herself so light-headed she could have flown out of the house on wings she didn't have and discovered her whole past life in a storyline she'd been denying from her earliest memories. Her parents, her sister, the children's home, her illness and operation, her parents' deaths, her sister's disappearance, her failed marriage, her new business venture, her meeting with Joe, up to that point of no return, or so it now seemed to her. And she laughed, as she'd never laughed before, ecstatically. Was life just a joke then, with all of us nothing more than prisoners of a prewritten destiny?

They spent the rest of that night in bed together, and Carol found Joe's predictions totally true: she'd never experienced such intense feelings of pleasure, far above mere sexuality, and she never wanted it to end. Joe had succeeded once again in his intentions towards her, although she only saw him now as her saviour and the mender of her broken heart. Blinded by what she thought of as the ultimate love, she gave herself to him totally, and forever, or so she believed.

Chapter 29

After that first night with Joe when she took her first dose of cocaine, Carol rapidly became addicted to the drug and was paying large sums to suppliers, through Joe's numerous contacts in that shady world. He would take her cash and bring back as much of the drug as she needed, without her realising how much she was actually spending now. The important thing for her was to have Joe in constant companionship and at hand for all her whims, whether material or sexual. She had no inkling that this was all part of his own long-term plan, to have her totally dependent upon him up to the point where he could legally take over all her finances, possibly becoming her official carer, and then eventually being awarded power of attorney.

But it was hardly the ideal life that she had at first imagined it would be. They argued a lot more as she became more dependent upon him and his drug contacts, and she would often lie prone on the settee staring at the ceiling and not giving a care for anything, including, of course, her magazine, which was falling into disrepute among her steady clients and advertisers.

Her ex-husband visited her sometimes and was alarmed to find her in such a state. He warned her once again about Joe and his true intentions, but she dismissed him as a fool who had never understood her need for an absolute love, which she had now discovered with Joe. Realising that she was now under the emprise of drugs and alcohol, he sadly left her alone then, hoping she would come to her senses one day and get rid of Joe once and for all before he totally ruined her.

The magazine eventually became such a burden, with declining numbers of issues sold and more advertisers pulling out, plus a hefty unpaid printer's bill, that she eventually decided to halt its publication and laid off all the staff she had gathered around her. She blamed Joe in part for its failure, although he denied any responsibility and told her bluntly that it was due to her own reliance now upon drugs and alcohol, which was nothing to do with him. He continued fleecing her accounts, both for her needs and his own, but she was too far gone and blinded by her love for him to see the truth. His plan appeared to be succeeding, and he knew how to play the game he'd begun with an inborn talent.

Carol's finances were rapidly decreasing. Her's and Joe's drug habit was costing a hefty sum each week, and nothing was coming in now the magazine had folded. At odd moments of lucidity, she realised that she needed to take some action to get her life back on track, and she told Joe that they should both stop using drugs, explaining her reasons. But he shrugged off her fears, telling her she was still wealthy enough for them to continue as they were, and later on he'd sort things out with the new deals he was setting up with his dealer friends. She knew it was wrong but was too deeply encrusted now to be able to pull out of her own will. That was also part of his long-term plan, and so she let it go on, powerless to do much about it on her own.

She knew intrinsically that continuing to use these drugs would lead to her financial ruin and might even eventually cause her death, and she wanted none of that. She remembered then how her mother had overthrown her alcohol problem by going into therapy for some time, while her daughters had been placed into temporary care, and so she considered that option for herself. The week she had spent in the mental hospital had done her the world of good, as she now recalled.

One morning then, when Joe was crashed out on the bed upstairs, unconscious with drugs, she looked up the number of a drug advisory group and called them. They explained the options available and invited her to meet with them for further help. She found that promising and arranged for a meeting over the following days.

When she did visit them a few days later, she spoke with one of the drug advisory personnel who ran the affair on a voluntary basis. His name was Barry, and he was an ex-drug addict himself who had managed to throw his habit and had been clean now for some years, so he knew all about the crises she was facing. He told her in explicit detail what the drugs would do to her mental and physical health if she didn't stop using them, and the fact that she had come to talk with him showed that she wanted to quit. He advised her to think really hard about all this, then return if she wanted them to help her overcome her habit. It would be difficult, of course, but he was the proof that it was feasible for her, as for anyone who truly wanted to stop using.

She left feeling a lot better and a lot more determined to stop using drugs, and on reaching home she told Joe about where she had been and what they had told her. She had decided not to take any more drugs in the future, because her business was now in tatters and her finances were in chaos, for which she blamed the drugs, if not him in person.

Joe then had a few moments of panic written across his face, but he quickly pulled himself together and told her that she needn't worry, he would always take care of her and make sure she never took more than she should, and she had seen for herself how much better life seemed when she was high and in his arms.

Weakened by stress and worry, she conceded that he was right in some respects, and so when he went to fetch some cocaine and offered to share it with her, she was unable to resist, as well he knew she would be. The danger had passed, and he played his games of lover and friend until any thought of rehabilitation had disappeared from her mind. He was still in total control, sadly for Carol, who succumbed once again to his wishes.

The following morning, feeling groggy and sipping a strong cup of tea while reproaching herself for being so weak and succumbing once again to Joe's manipulations, she received a letter on which she at once recognized Elizabeth's handwriting on the envelope. Surprised, she stared hard at the envelope a few minutes, as though in shock. Could her long-lost sister really have sent her a letter after all this time? Her hands trembled as she opened it and read:

'My dear Carol

I know this letter will be a huge surprise after so long, but I hope it will find you well and happy, as well as our poor mother, who must also be wondering what happened to me after I left the convent. I must apologise for not staying in touch with you both, but I went through so many emotional shocks and crises concerning my future as a nun and whether I was really cut out for such a life. In the end I realised that I wasn't, and it took a friendship with a man to teach me this.

To cut a long story short, as mum used to say, I left the convent and I married that same man, Sid, and we moved away to Northampton to begin a new life of our own. And we now have two lovely daughters, Penny and Rebecca, your nieces and mum's grandchildren, as if I had copied a pattern that mum had lived through with our dad and us, a kind of prewritten destiny in a way.

The reason I have now decided to write this letter to you rather than to mum is so that we can perhaps meet sometime soon and talk things over about our lives and what has happened since we all parted. I think it might come as too much of a shock to mum, so I'd prefer to hear from you and meet you first and then take it from there. I hope you won't mind. I really don't want to be apart from either of you any longer.

If you don't want to meet me after so long a time, I will understand, although it will be painful for me and my family. I often talk about you both to them all, and they are longing to meet and know you as well. I'd also like to know how you have been getting on since we last saw each other. I hope things have worked out for you as well as they have for me.

I know you will think me awful for not contacting you before, but when I decided to leave the convent, I wasn't sure how you would take it, because I knew that you were against me entering *the convent and becoming a nun from the start, but that's all over now and I'm living my life as best I can.*

If you want to contact me, I have included my address and telephone number in this letter. And I do look forward to hearing from you and so will wait patiently for your reply.

Your loving sister,

Elizabeth.'

Carol sat and read the letter several times. She felt overwhelmed and uncertain, although she knew deep down at once that she must reach out to Elizabeth. Her mother would have wanted this. And to think that her sister had no idea that their mother had passed away some time ago now. It was her duty then to inform her of at least that much.

When Joe shambled bleary-eyed into the kitchen much later, she told him about the letter she'd received from her long-lost sister, which had really made her happy. Surprised and slightly annoyed, he read the letter slowly, frowning, and then asked her what she planned to do, and if she really wanted to meet up with her sister again after so many years.

He was immediately worried, of course, that Elizabeth would come back permanently onto the scene and so interfere with his own relationship with Carol, upsetting all his long-term plans and scheming. He wasn't keen on letting that happen, although again Carol suspected nothing.

"After all this time, do you really think it's a good idea to meet your sister again?" he asked gruffly.

"What do you mean?" Carol replied.

"Well, I know you both have memories from a shared past, like us at the kids' home we were in together, but I'm not sure it would be a good thing to dig all that up again, now we've all moved on and grown up. And she obviously has a good and settled life now with her own family, so why would she want to be in touch again after so long?"

"But she doesn't even know that our mother is dead, nor anything that has happened to me and my marriage and all that, so I think I should at least let her know that much, don't you? She took the trouble to write to me, so the least I can do is write back..."

Joe shrugged his shoulders and threw the letter back at her nastily.

"Oh, what do I care anyway," he shouted. "It's your bloody family, not mine, so do what you like...you never think about me and what I'm feeling so I don't care anymore..."

He stormed out then, grabbing his coat and slamming the front door. Carol heard the car being started then screeching off in a burst of skidding tyres. Exasperated, but also saddened by his reaction, she conjured up enough strength and willpower to write a return letter to Elizabeth, feeling that it was important, especially having witnessed Joe's paranoic reaction. Elizabeth was the only remaining family she had, while Joe was something else and getting worse by the day.

She sat down calmly then and wrote a letter to Elizabeth:

'My dearest Elizabeth,

Thank you so much for your wonderful letter. It was a huge surprise, of course, but I was so pleased to hear from you after so long, and after so much has happened in both our lives. I thought it was better to write to you rather than telephoning right away, even if I am still sorely tempted to do so, just to hear your voice again.

I was so glad to hear that you are happy in your new life, and I think it would be great if we meet sometime very soon. I would absolutely love to meet your husband and your two children, and I can hardly believe that I have two nieces. I look forward to getting to know them.

But I also have some very sad news for you, Elizabeth. Our dear mother passed away a few years ago now. I tried so hard to find you at the time to let you know so that you could attend the funeral, but nobody knew where you had gone, and no-one we asked had any idea of your whereabouts. But rest assured, mum was pleased to know that you had found happiness after leaving the convent, and she would have been so pleased to know she had two grandchildren. I'm sure she's watching over them, and you, from wherever she is, so don't feel too badly about all this. I'll explain more about it all when we do meet.

I will telephone you soon and then we can arrange to meet somewhere. You will always be welcome to come to my house. I got divorced from my husband a few years ago, but now I have partner, Joseph, who was at the convent home when we were, so you should remember him, the boy I was always talking with apart from all the others. I met him again by hazard, and we've been together for some time now. But we can chat about all of that when we do meet. I am so looking forward to hearing all about your life.

So please do stay in touch, I will call soon, and then we can meet whenever you want. Just let me know. We are family, and we shouldn't forget that now.

All my love,

Your sister, Carol.

Joe, meanwhile, had returned to the house and again slammed doors and went skulking into the living room. Carol had just sealed the envelope and wanted to post her letter right away.

"Joe, could you drive me to the post office," she calmly asked. "I'd like to post this letter right away…"

"Ha, you think I'm your bloody chauffeur as well now, do you?" he retorted, and she saw that he'd just taken a dose of cocaine.

She left him, angry inside but not wanting to row with him again. She would walk herself to the post office. Elizabeth suddenly meant so much more to her than this angry man who was so often out of his head now with drugs and drink. She seemed to ignore the fact that it was her car anyway, and that she could have simply driven herself to the town centre. Leaving him in his dispossessed state, she took the bus into town and posted her precious letter with joy. Perhaps things might really change for the better now at last.

Chapter 30

Carol was once again sinking deeper into a chronic depression and suffering from a new sense of loneliness, as Joe didn't seem to be supporting her much anymore and he was more often out and about the town than at home with her. The initial magic of their renewed relationship had soon faded to become another of her many lost dreams, and that pained her inside more than she could bear. She had no idea of what he was up to when he was out with his so-called friends and work partners, although she did have deep suspicions now, as the flow of drugs through Joe and her home was constant. But as she was still under the emprise of drugs herself, she couldn't even think about tackling Joe and his shady lifestyle.

In this state of mind, she decided one morning to telephone to her old friend Kimberley, who'd worked with her on the magazine as photographer and art director, although she had been laid off as abruptly as all the other staff when Carol had become involved with Joe again. But they'd been friends since working together at the supermarket, and she had always been able to talk with her about all her problems, and vice versa. Now, she was hoping for some moral and friendly support from Kimberley, who was very sensible and supportive.

"Hi, Kimberley...it's Carol..." she said softly into the receiver.

"Well, that *is* a surprise!" Kimberley replied in a slightly sarcastic tone. "I thought you'd finished with all of us when you kicked us out of the magazine job..."

Taken aback by this response, Carol was dumbstruck for a moment. She hadn't been expecting this at all.

"But...it wasn't my fault," she stuttered, scrambling for words and trying to get her thoughts back on track. "Things just seemed to get out of hand, you understand?"

"Oh, yes, I understand, as we all do now..."

"What do you mean?"

"Well, that Joe chap you hitched up with, he's hardly the sweet darling boy you seem to think he is, on the contrary. We all had to put up with his moving into your life and taking it over, while you sat swooning at his falseness and trickery. We could all see it, but Peter was the first, and he warned us all about what was going on, but you were blinded by all that Joe's sweet talk and promises, I guess. Then we all had to suffer the consequences, out of work just like that with no warning, but the magazine could have been huge by now if you hadn't gone down that slippery road with him..."

"What do you mean?"

"Oh, Carol, come on, we've known each other long enough not to beat about the bush, haven't we? That Joe is one of the most notorious drug dealers in the town, and I know he's got you hooked as well, as Peter told us everything that was going on after he visited you a few times..."

This was all so unexpected, Carol was again struck speechless. Did the whole world know about Joe then, more than she did? It suddenly seemed that way, and she felt a dark shadow creeping up on her as she struggled to reply to Kimberley, whom she had considered to be a true friend, one of the very few left to her.

"But it'll be all right soon," she stuttered, confused. "I know I made a lot of mistakes, and I am sorry, really. I'm looking at going into rehab now anyway, and then I might get the magazine going again if you'd be interested..."

"Ah, no, I hardly think so, Carol...You seem to forget that I'm on my own now with a young daughter to bring up, and I won't be messed about like that again...I'm sorry, but I'd rather you didn't contact me again in the future, as I've got my own life back on track and can't be dealing with anyone else's problems..."

And with that, she hung up, leaving Carol absolutely devastated. She had always considered Kimberley to be one of her closest friends, and they had worked up a great relationship during the years they'd worked together, often spending time together and socialising after work. They had lost touch briefly when Carol had got married and left the supermarket, and then Kimberley too had met someone with whom she had a daughter. Then Carol's magazine endeavour had brought them together again for a few happy and productive months.

But now, all that was as nothing, apparently, and it left Carol heartbroken once again. Why was her world crumbling around her while she looked meekly on? She never once blamed herself for her actions, as if often the case in such tragic cases. The world was to blame, while she was the innocent victim. But she did recognise the need for her to change dramatically, if she wanted to get her life back on track. And the first step would be to break her dependence on drugs.

Calming down gradually, she made herself a coffee and sat in the kitchen awhile, reflecting on what her life had become without her truly realising it. That was, she told herself, a first step towards a solution, accepting her own responsibility. She recalled the happy moments she'd spent together with Joe at the children's home, when they were little more than children looking out at the grand highway of life stretching out before them, and that aura of innocent tenderness returned to sweeten the hurt she was now feeling because of how Joe had turned out.

But surely, if she could change her own life around by going into rehab and restarting her business, Joe could do the same if he chose to do so? She made a mental note to talk about this with him when he came back. Because he always did come back, as she now realised. She didn't know why, but at least he did come back, and she clung to that fact as to a lifebelt in a turbulent ocean.

Later that same day, she thought it would be a good idea to call her sister, Elizabeth, who would have by now received her letter and be aware of her own situation and their mother's death. She felt certain that Elizabeth would be understanding and compassionate towards her and her problems, and she felt a desperate need to talk with her, and eventually meet with her again very soon.

"Hello, Elizabeth? It's me, Carol…"

"Oh, hello, Carol! How wonderful to hear your voice again…" Elizabeth replied in a joyful tone. "I got your letter, and we've been talking about you ever since. Both Sid and the girls can't wait to meet you…"

"That is nice to hear," Carol told, feeling suddenly placated towards the world and her own troubles. "I can't wait to meet you all as well and talk with you about all that's happened since we went our separate ways. I was a bit worried you wouldn't want to see me again after the news I had to give you…"

"Ah, you mean about mum…? Yes, that did upset me, but I'd rather we talk about that when we do meet rather than on the telephone. We can both catch up then on what we've been doing after so many years of being apart. Is that all right?"

"Yes, of course, don't worry, I understand."

"We'd like to visit you first, if that's okay, so my family can get to know you and the place I grew up in, as well as the convent, of course…What do you think?"

"That would be lovely," Carol replied, caught off guard a little. She'd have preferred going to visit her sister and family away from her house and Joe. "But my house is being decorated and converted a bit at the moment, so you'd have to put up with all that, I'm afraid…"

"Oh, that doesn't matter, Carol, we want to see you and be with you for a bit, we have such a lot to talk about on both sides, I guess."

"Yes, we certainly do…but I can cook a nice lunch, and we can spend the day together, and maybe wander a bit around the town and show your family the places we knew as kids…"

"Sounds great, Carol. So, let's fix a day for next week, shall we?"

"All right…"

"The weekend would be best for us, because of the girls going to school and Sid at work…will that be okay with you?"

Yes, of course…so let's say Saturday, shall we?"

"All right…I'll get it arranged my end, and we'll come as early as we can to have the whole day with you…"

"That'll be fantastic. Thank you, Elizabeth, I really am looking forward to seeing you again…"

"Me too…"

Carol felt a new spark of hope after speaking with Elizabeth, convinced she had done the right thing in calling her. Sisters often had silent understandings and depth of thought unique to their standing as siblings, and this had always been the case with them, or so she now told herself. They were, in truth, as different in character as chalk and cheese, but now Carol needed Elizabeth's understanding and comfort, and for the rest of that day she was in a much lighter mood, if not actually happy. She felt grateful for once that Joe wasn't around. She would have to deal with him again, she knew, when she informed him that her sister was going to visit her. But she knew she was right, and nothing would put her off now. Not even Joe and his wicked machinations.

Chapter 31

Joe was becoming ever more embroiled with the people supplying him with cocaine, a small gang of dealers who were a branch of a large international cartel, and who ran their business locally. Now they had him solidly hooked and deeply in debt to them, it was easy for them to manipulate him and use him for their own ends, selling and distributing and collecting money owed. He was soon known locally then as a reliable supplier to users in the area.

He also made sure that Carol remained dependent upon the drugs he stashed at her house, because he knew then that she would be under his control and thus allow him unlimited access to her assets. He realised that the people he was now involved with could be ruthless when they had to be and wouldn't tolerate any high debt or small theft of their products, and so he was playing a dangerous game by using their products to satisfy his and Carol's addictions. But the attraction and ease of being able to use the drugs pushed the inherent danger to the back of his mind, and he told himself that with Carol's wealth behind him he would always manage to pay it back when the need arose.

Carol didn't know what he was really up to when he was away from her, sometimes for days on end, because he never told her anything about his private life. He had her where he wanted her now, totally under his domination and in love with him, or so she believed, which lent him a free hand for the other side of his life. His original plan with Carol was coming to fruition a lot faster and better than he had hoped, and that egged him on to continue further.

There were still frequent rows and problems between the two of them, following which he would storm out of the house and go and stay with his friend named Jacob, who lived in a flat not far from Carol's house. He would always take her car, as she hadn't driven it for some time, and he considered it to be his.

But after she told him that her sister and family were going to visit them, he saw a new crisis looming. He hadn't paid much attention when Carol showed him Elizabeth's letter, but on reflection, he realised that this could mean trouble on the horizon. The last thing he needed was for Carol's family to interfere with his own plans, and he set to thinking about a solution. It wouldn't be easy.

"Don't you think it would be nice if we went away together for a couple of days somewhere before your sister comes to see you?" he suggested one morning.

Carol was surprised, to say the least, and it took her a moment to digest what he'd said. But then she saw him looking fondly at her as they drank their coffee, and she knew she couldn't resist once again.

"That would be nice," she replied with a smile. "Where did you have in mind?"

"Anywhere you fancy. Not too far away, of course..."

"What about Ramsgate? We used to go there as kids with mum and dad, and it would be nice to go and see what it's like now..."

"Okay, Ramsgate it is, then. Can I ask you to book a hotel and all that, though? I have to pop out now and see someone, so..."

"All right," Carol agreed, hiding as best she could her disappointment. She hoped that being alone with him in another place might bring him back closer again.

A couple of days later they set off together for Ramsgate, with Joe driving Carol's car as usual. He appeared to be in a pleasant mood, and they had only taken a small dose of the drugs they used constantly before setting off. That was pleasant for Carol, who watched the landscape flash by, taking her back to her childhood days, before the string of tragedy came to trip her up with the other members of her family. Life wasn't fair, she knew that now, but it still had its joyful moments.

They stayed at a small but pleasant hotel, and again Joe seemed to be playing the game of devoted friend and lover again, making Carol feel at ease and happy. The weather was warm and pleasant, and they spent an afternoon on the beach, with Joe swimming vigorously in the sea while Carol watched with pleasure. If only he was always like this, she thought, knowing it wouldn't last and that they'd return home to start again the endless cycle of arguments and loneliness. A bleak prospect, but she quickly pushed it out of her thoughts. Live for the moment, she told herself, watching Joe battle against the waves.

They spent a pleasant couple of hours together in their room then, again restraining their drug use to a minimum, and Joe seemed tender and attentive towards Carol, as he had been at the beginning of their relationship, reassuring her of his love and friendship and grateful for all she had done for him. She fell for his act completely again, amazed at the sudden change while hoping that it would last when they returned home.

"I don't want things to change," he told her then out of the blue. "I mean, between us and everything at home…"

"Why would it change?" Carol asked, surprised.

"Well, you know, with your sister coming to visit and all that…I wouldn't want her to come and interfere with us at all…"

"Oh, Joe, she'd never do that," Carol told him with a smile. "She was always the good girl, that's true, if you can remember her at the home? And she became a nun before she got married, but now she's married with kids and just like the rest of us, so you needn't worry about her interfering in our lives. She just wants to make contact again, like I do…"

"I hope so," he said bluntly. "I won't put up with anyone interfering in my affairs, you know that don't you?"

"Of course I do, so stop worrying about it. It'll be fine, you'll see…"

They left things at that point and went out for a meal to a chic restaurant, appearing to be like any normal loving couple on a short holiday. But they were both drinking heavily, beer and then wine, becoming quickly inebriated, and at one point Joe disappeared into the toilets for quite a long while and Carol knew why, of course. He was unable to resist the call of his habit, even though she had done so for the whole of that day. Disappointed, she tried hard to keep her spirits up, but she feared the worst was still to come. And she was right about that.

He started to kick off when he returned to the table, and she saw the obvious signs of what he had been doing, the traces of white powder, the far-away look in his glazed eyes, his drawling as he spoke. He raised his voice and accused her of drinking too much wine, and she was obviously becoming an alcoholic despite all the attention he paid to her, and carried on in that vein for some time, while other guests and the staff were looking on askance, wondering what had happened and what was going on.

"You dragged me here under false pretences," he shouted then. "Playing a game of all lovey-dovey and in reality, you want shot of me, I know, I'm not stupid..."

"Oh, Joe, don't be like that, you know it's not true. Remember how nice it was together earlier and how we both enjoyed ourselves on the beach and back at the hotel..."

"Just a game!" he retorted. "And if you think you can pull the wool over my eyes you're mistaken, my girl, I can tell you that much. Well, I've had enough now, anyway, so you can make your own bloody way home again. If that's the way you want to play things, I'm off..."

He stormed out of the restaurant, leaving Carol speechless and in tears, not knowing what she'd done to provoke him so violently. Things had appeared to be fine between them since they left home that morning, but obviously they weren't. The very things he was accusing her off were all his own actions as far as she could tell, and she was devastated once more at how she'd been treated. She settled the bill and hurried back to the hotel, hoping to find Joe there in a calmed state, or perhaps asleep, if she were lucky.

But he wasn't there. Nor were his things. Her car had also gone from the hotel carpark. He'd deserted her, left her alone, and she didn't know what to do to lessen her pain and get her life back on track once and for all. Joe was untenable, she realised that now, but too late. She cried herself to sleep and then woke in fits and starts throughout the night, knowing what she ought to do – what she must do in fact – if ever she wanted to be herself again. Her real self.

She returned home the following day by train, arriving late afternoon. Joe wasn't at home, nor was her car. She felt relieved in a way, as she wouldn't have been able to handle another violent confrontation. But at the same time, her heart throbbed for his touch, his moods, what she imagined was his love for her, above all the rest. But she also knew that now was the moment for her to decide, to remove him from her home and her life, if ever she wanted to get back to normal.

"I will ask him to leave when he does come back," she told herself then, feeling strong all of a sudden. "If I don't, I think he'll destroy me completely."

She slept then, exhausted by what she'd been through. She was suffering with a massive hangover and withdrawal symptoms, and so slept fitfully through the night.

The next day she got a call from him, apologising and telling her how upset he was at what he had done. He asked if he could come to see her and make things up with her again, and she was unable to say no, of course.

"I'll bring something to make you happy and forget about all that happened…" he told her then, and she knew what he meant.

She admonished herself for being so weak but felt helpless now when faced with his far-fetched promises that never got realised, but she ached for his arms around her, the comfort he secured for her, even with the drugs she knew would settle all their disputes. That's how it was, and perhaps always would be.

Chapter 32

The day came when she was expecting the visit of her sister Elizabeth and her family. She went out of her way to make sure the house was clean and tidy, and started preparing the special lunch she'd planned for them. They could have gone out to a restaurant, of course, but she preferred to spend as much time as was possible with Elizabeth at home, where they could talk more easily and confidentially. They certainly had a great deal to discuss, as Carol well knew and feared a little.

Joe looked on at her preparations with a somewhat hostile eye, and she knew he wasn't looking forward to the visit. She asked him if he'd be at home when they arrived and if he'd join them for lunch. He told her then that he had to meet some people for his work and things and so he wouldn't be around at lunchtime, but he'd try to be back in the late afternoon. Carol was a little disappointed but also relieved in a way. She dreaded the thought of Joe becoming aggressive or violent under the influence of drugs, and she didn't want Elizabeth to know anything about that side of her life. Much better then that Joe wouldn't be around. He went out shortly after that.

Elizabeth and her family arrived as planned, and Carol remarked how they pulled up outside in what looked to be a new car. She was impressed and rushed out to meet them. She felt a little nervous and didn't know what to expect, meeting her sister again after so many years of separation. She recognised her straight away, the inborn softness of her face and her eyes that had always made her the virtuous member of the family, long before she'd ever contemplated joining a convent.

"Hello!" she exclaimed as Elizabeth got out of the car and rushed to embrace her. "I'm glad you made it okay…"

"Hello, Carol," Elizabeth said in return as they hugged each other warmly an instant. "Great to see you again, and to be back here…"

She then introduced Carol to her husband, Sid, and to Penny and Rebecca, her two young daughters. She thought at once what a neat and perfect family they appeared to be, all smiling and happy to be together, although she wasn't surprised really, knowing what a serene character Elizabeth was in her own self. It was normal that this had rubbed off onto her family. Whereas in her own case…well, she refused to even think about it on that special day.

There was such a lot for them to discuss and catch up with on both sides, and neither knew where to begin. But Elizabeth had noticed right away that Carol didn't look well; she had a strained look on her face and in her blurry eyes, and that worried her. She remembered seeing a very similar look on their mother's face when she'd been drinking too much shortly before going into rehab and placing them both in the children's home. Was Carol suffering from the same type of problem, she wondered. She made a mental note to mention this later when they were alone and able to talk about all that had happened since their last meeting. Which was a lot, as they both knew.

Lunch was quite a pleasant affair for all of them, as Carol had thought of the children and had bought pizza and burgers, while the adults had roast chicken and trimmings, almost like a Sunday lunch, although it was Saturday. She put a bottle of wine on the table, and they toasted the coming together of the two sisters again, although Carol barely touched hers, sipping at it now and again despite the huge urge she suffered to down it all in one go and refill her glass. She knew she mustn't give way to those urges while Elizabeth was there, and she felt a lot better in herself for this. She was glad also that Joe hadn't turned up to spoil things.

After lunch, Elizabeth said she'd help Carol with the washing-up as that would give them a chance to talk and catch up on all the things they still had to tell each other. Sid and the girls sat in the lounge and watched a video.

First off, Carol told Elizabeth all about their mother's death, and what had caused it. She had started drinking again, more and more as time passed, and Carol felt that she was concealing some dreadful secret she felt unable to talk about with her. She was convinced it was something to do with the fact that she couldn't have children, and no doubt related to the operation she'd undergone while still at the home. Something didn't sit right, and it haunted Carol all the time now. Sometimes she felt responsible for her mother's death, although she knew she wasn't, but that guilt hovered incessantly over her, and that had caused her to start drinking as well.

"I noticed you weren't looking too good," Elizabeth told her then. "Are you still drinking too much now?"

"Sometimes, yes...I try not to, but it's hard, especially with Joe, who loves his drink as well, you understand..."

"And he came back on the scene after you got divorced, then?" Elizabeth asked.

"Oh, yes, a long time afterwards...there was another man, Peter, who worked on the magazine with me, but he was already married with kids so that didn't go anywhere..."

"And the magazine? What happened with that?"

"I'm not sure...it just sort of lost its way when Peter left, and then Joe wasn't up to the job, and things got worse and worse, so I decided to stop it before it ruined me completely..."

"And Joe in all of that? What does he do for a living now?

Carol felt a panic growing, and she really didn't want to talk about Joe, and certainly not about the reality of her situation.

"I'm not really sure," she replied. "A bit of this and that, odd jobs in building and stuff, and he travels around a lot."

"Using your car?"

"Yes, since I don't need it much now I'm not working any more..."

Elizabeth was quick to put things together, reading Carol's face like a book. But she didn't want an open confrontation, as that was the last thing Carol needed right then. But she was worried about her sister and felt that she must do something to help her as soon as she could. They had lost their mother tragically, and she had no wish to lose her sister in the same way. She already suspected that Carol was using drugs as well as over-drinking, and that was a another huge worry, but she thought it better not to confront her right away. She was also very concerned about the hold Joe seemed to be exerting over her. But how to talk calmly about all that now, with her own family waiting for them in the sitting room.

"You must try to sort yourself out a bit, Carol," she told her then. "Don't go down the same route our mother took, please. I'm here now and I'll always be on hand if you need me, so please don't hesitate to call me..."

"Thank you, Elizabeth. It's true what you say, and I do need some help. But let's talk about it again a bit later, shall we? Your family's waiting..."

They hugged closely an instant, and Carol sensed her sister's warmth and strength of character flooding into her own body and felt comforted. If only this had happened long before, she thought, before Joe had come back into my life.

Just as they went back into the sitting room, Joe, as though on cue, came bursting through the front door, obviously much the worse for drink. Carol's heart dropped and she found it difficult even to look at him, but she pulled herself together and introduced him to Elizabeth and her family.

"Oh, I remember you at the children's home," he told Elizabeth in a slurred voice. "Do you remember me?"

"Yes, of course. You used to talk with Carol all the time, and everyone said you were a perfect couple since neither of you were very happy and spent most of your time together..."

"True," Joe agreed. "And you were the little angel, I remember, always praying in the chapel and running about with the sisters and praying and all that crap..."

"Joe!" Carol interrupted. "Show some respect, will you!"

"Don't worry," Elizabeth told her. "We all know he doesn't mean it, do you, Joe? You were always the rebel, even back then..."

"Well, I'm all right now, anyway" he drawled. "And I'm taking care of your sister now, so you needn't go worrying about her..."

"Yes, I've heard a bit about that...."

They stared at each other, and in that instant Joe realised that Elizabeth was aware of a lot of things, and that Carol had obviously told her far too much already. That didn't please him, and he read in Elizabeth's eyes that she didn't care for him at all. She wasn't easily fooled, and he would have to be careful if he didn't want to upset the boat he was sailing in with Carol's blessing.

He shrugged his shoulders and went stomping upstairs to the bedroom, slamming the door after him. An awkward silence ensued, and the friendly atmosphere seemed to have been broken. Carol felt livid inside, but she didn't want to go down that road right then with Joe. He was ruining her life, as she now knew, and this was one more step along that path as far as she was concerned. Elizabeth had understood everything.

"Well, so much for your Joe," she said softly. "I really think you should change your life, Carol, and as soon as you can. We'll help you, won't we Sid, so don't hesitate to call us if you need us. I can see that you're not well and you're not happy, so you must change..."

"I'll try," Carol replied. "I do want to change, really...I need to tell you so much more, but now with him upstairs it's not easy, you understand?"

"Well, why don't you come and stay with us for a couple of days next week, and we can talk as much as you want. What do you say?"

"You mean it? Oh, that would be lovely, really...but I don't want to impose..."

"Rubbish! That's settled, you let me know when and we'll arrange it our end, okay?"

"Yes, Okay. And thank you, Elizabeth. I really needed to see you again; I understand that now."

"Good. We'll help you sort things out, don't worry...but don't bring him with you, will you?"

"No, of course not...he wouldn't come anyway, knowing him..."

The rest of the day passed peacefully enough, as Joe remained unconscious in the bedroom. They went for a short walk around the town, reminiscing, reliving their childhood, and Elizabeth felt moved on seeing the convent and the home again, although she resisted the urge to go in and talk with the sisters. All that was another lifetime away, and she couldn't go back, she knew. Destiny had taken her far away, and now she held hands with her destiny in the forms of her husband and children, plus her newfound sister again. Wasn't that enough for them all? She sincerely hoped it would be.

Carol and Elizabeth left Sid and the girls in a games arcade for a short time and went together to visit the cemetery in which their mother was buried. Elizabeth asked to do this, as she hadn't attended the funeral and was feeling a slight guilt over this, even though she really had nothing to reproach herself with, apart from her prolonged disappearance.

The grave appeared neglected, as Carol hadn't visited it for some time now. She'd placed a marble headstone with their mother's details inscribed, so that was something, Elizabeth told herself. They bought some flowers at the florists near the entrance and posed them in the vase, clearing away the weeds and the dead flowers. It was a solemn moment for each of them; both lost in their own thoughts.

"Did she suffer much?" Elizabeth asked then as they left the cemetery.

"I don't think so," Carol replied. "She didn't really know what was going on according to the doctor's report. It was just so tragic, her drinking so much again after so long being cured and happy with her work."

"It's a bit like destiny always leading us on," Elizabeth said then, thoughtful.

"Do you really believe that?"

"Yes, I do...you know, I was convinced I was going to spend the rest of my life as a nun, and then Sid came along and everything changed in my eyes...so we can never be certain that what we choose will last for always..."

"I understand," Carol told her. "I was the same, until Joe came back into my life...and I met him at the convent as well, remember..."

"So, we're not that different then," Elizabeth said. "And all our destinies are related to who we are and what happened to us while growing up...strange, though, don't you think?"

"Yes, I do. There was divinity in you, virtue in our mother's struggle to keep us safe, and now destiny has brought us together here at her grave...it seems all to have been written by someone else and we just have to live it..."

"Well, I'm glad we came here anyway. I needed to say a prayer for her right here. And I'm glad we're together again."

"And so am I..."

They left the graveside then and returned to Elizabeth's happy family. That was her safeguard now, as she well knew.

That night, after returning to her home, she prayed devoutly on behalf of Carol and her seemingly overpowering problems. Would prayer be enough though, or would it take more drastic action to set Carol free once and for all in a life she could enjoy every moment of? Only time would tell, and she hoped that they would find enough time to achieve it all soon.

Back in her home, Carol sat alone, reflecting on the day's events. She was delighted to have met and talked with Elizabeth and her family. She felt the sincerity in Elizabeth's regard and words, and she knew what she must do next. Joe would no longer run her life as he wished, and that was a firm resolution. For the rest, she would try to be strong until the time was ripe to act.

Elizabeth's family had shown her everything that was missing in her own life, and she was determined then to follow that same path. She eventually fell asleep on the sofa, dreaming of her family and ignoring the drunken man upstairs asleep in her bed.

Chapter 33

Carol visited Elizabeth as arranged the following week and stayed overnight, leaving a disgruntled Joe by himself in her home. He disapproved of Carol going away alone, mainly because he feared her telling the truth about his set up in Carol's home to outsiders. But Carol ignored his ranting and left, traveling by train and leaving her car for him to use, one concession he refused to give up, and so it was easier for her t to simply agree.

Carol opened her heart completely to Elizabeth, allowing everything to pour out in a flood: Joe's emprise over her, his use of drugs and how he'd started her own addiction, his involvement with drug gangs and other criminals, and how he was depleting her finances without a care in the world or any thoughts about their future, or more exactly, her future.

Elizabeth listened, horrified. She'd had suspicions following her visit to Carol and meeting Joe briefly, and now they were confirmed. But she was also very practical and down to earth, having been taught at the convent to deal with crises, and so she laid out plans for Carol to free herself from Joe's influence and the world he moved in, because if she didn't, he would drag her down with him, and heaven knows where she might end up. At best, it might be prison as an accessory, as she was harbouring a criminal as well as his stash of drugs and illicit money. At worst, well, Carol knew herself what she meant.

It was all a huge shock, but Carol knew that she alone held the key to regain her total freedom from such influences. She agreed to let Elizabeth help with getting access to some sort of rehabilitation, and also to keep an eye on her financial situation, until such time that she was rid of Joe and could build up some kind of business venture that would help get her back into a comfort zone. She trusted Elizabeth implicitly, and when she left to return home, she felt uplifted and determined to see it through. Enough was enough, and she had had more than enough now.

When she arrived back home Joe was absent, and she felt relieved. She didn't want any confrontation right then, as she needed to digest everything she'd planned with Elizabeth and then set it all into action, and rapidly. No more wasting time now, she told herself, and that was definite.

That same evening, someone rang her doorbell. Curious, she went to open it and was surprised to see Peter standing there, a sheepish grin on his face.

"Hello, Carol," he said warmly. "I was in the area, and so thought I'd call by to see how things are with you now…"

"Peter!" she exclaimed. "This *is* a surprise. Please…come in…"

They sat opposite each other in the living room and talked nonstop for quite some time, relating their adventures since parting ways. Carol learnt that Peter was now divorced, but he saw his children regularly. He'd built up his own business with a car dealership and was doing very well, employing several mechanics and drivers for private hire occasions. Then he asked Carol what she'd been up to since they last met, and how her business was going.

Carol looked startled for a moment. She would have loved to pour her heart out to this man, who'd always been kind and understanding with her, and whom she knew still harboured romantic feelings towards her, but she felt ashamed of everything that had happened to her since he'd gone out of her life. How different things might be now if they'd remained together, she thought.

She told him that she was still living with Joe, and that things had gone from bad to worse over time. Joe had proved himself useless from the start when taking over Peter's job as sales manager, and eventually the magazine had folded. Then she'd discovered that Joe was involved with a lot of shady underworld figures who kept him under surveillance and obliged him to work for them in all kinds of illegal business, and she was totally at a loss now what to do for the best.

"But that's just awful," Peter said, concerned. "Can't you just ask him to leave?"

"Oh, it's not that simple," Carol told him with a sigh. "He got me hooked as well, and he never listens to a word I say now. But my sister Elizabeth has contacted me again, and I've just come back from seeing her, and together we're going to sort things out now…"

"Well, that's good to know…and if I can be of any assistance, you just have to ask, really…"

"Thank you, Peter. It is good to see you and talk with you again…but I dread to think what Joe might say or do if he comes back and finds you here alone with me…I don't know where he is, you understand?"

"Of course...but why don't we go out for a drink or a meal together, if you're up to it, that is..."

"That would be lovely," Carol replied, meaning it. "But I don't think I could drink any wine right now, to be frank. I must stop drinking now to be able to handle all the rest in my life..."

"Don't worry, I understand. In fact, I also gave up drinking some time ago, so we can both have tonic water or orange juice, or whatever you fancy," Peter chuckled.

"Fine...give me ten minutes to powder my nose, would you..."

"Of course, no rush..."

They drove to a nearby restaurant in Peter's car and had a pleasant meal and conversation. The topic of the magazine inevitably came up, and Carol admitted that she'd love to be able to restart it one day but wasn't sure if she'd ever be up to it again. Peter encouraged her as best he could, but he could see how depressed and downcast she appeared to be. He changed the subject.

Deep inside, he was seething inwardly against Joe and what he'd done to Carol, because he saw at once that he was to blame for everything that had gone wrong with her life since he'd left her and his job. Perhaps if he'd stayed with her, she would still be the bright young woman he'd fallen in love with. Now, she seemed like a wreck of her former self, and he blamed himself a little for this. But how to fight against your destiny when it becomes ruthless and choices have to be made? He had also learnt the lessons the hard way.

They drove back to Carol's place after the meal, and she invited him in for a coffee. They found Joe lounging in the sitting room, drinking a beer, which was a bit of a shock, but he seemed affable enough and happy to hear that Carol had been out for a meal with Peter.

But Peter told them abruptly that he had to leave, some business to attend to, and wished them a good evening. He couldn't bear to look at Joe's cynical attitude, knowing how badly he'd been treating Carol.

"Goodbye, Peter," Carol said, a little put out by Joe's unexpected presence. "It was lovely to see you again…"

"We'll have to do it again then some time," Peter replied. "If you don't object, Joe…"

"Not at all, mate," Joe drawled with a half-smile. "I'm always busy with my business associates nowadays and Carol loves going out, so feel free…"

Carol saw Peter out, and he told her that he'd love to see her again if she agreed, and they could go out anywhere she chose."

"Just call me beforehand," he told her. "And preferably when he's not around, eh?"

He kissed her chastely on the cheek and she watched him drive away.

Joe stayed silent when she went back in, ruminating something or other no doubt in his confused state, and she decided to go to bed, She didn't want him forcing drink or drugs upon her again, nor ever. That much she'd decided with force now after meeting Elizabeth and then Peter, two staunch allies from her past.

Chapter 34

Back home, all Peter could think about was Carol, and he was more than happy to have contacted her again. But he was deeply alarmed by the changes he'd seen in her appearance and manner, and that was a worry. He asked himself then if it really had been a wise decision to have contacted her again out of the blue, although he knew deep down the true reasons for that decision. It was as though something stronger than reality had pushed him into it, and he told himself that she needed him more than ever before. That became his justification, if ever he still needed one.

He'd realised at once that Joe was to blame for all that had gone wrong in her life. When he'd left her employment and she'd apparently chosen Joe over him as companion, he'd been hurt and a little peeved at her, for sure. But now, having lived alone for so long and wondering where his own happiness had gone, he saw that his troubles were inexistant compared with what she was now living through. That other man had turned out exactly as he'd predicted he would to himself at the time, and he felt a duty now towards Carol, one that he wished to fulfil. He would help her, no matter what, and having seen her and talked with her again added to his determination.

He took out a photo from his wallet, one he'd kept carefully since he'd left Carol. It was a portrait of herself she'd given him, and now, as he stared longingly at it, he could see how much she had changed, in appearance and character. Again, Joe stood out as the culprit, and he knew what he must do to end her unliveable situation.

Later that night he sent her an e-mail, wanting to let her know that he was on her side, if she still wanted him to be:

'My dear Carol,

It was lovely to see you again, and I want to thank you for our evening together, almost like old times. But I was alarmed to hear about your problems with Joe and all that, and I am willing to help you in any way I can, if you allow it. So, I hope we can meet again very soon and enjoy each other's company a bit, because I need such a friendship as well, so please don't hesitate to contact me whenever you want to. I await your reply with impatience!

Your true friend, with lots of love, Peter'.

There was no response the next morning when he checked, and that was disappointing. But he told himself that she probably didn't check her e-mails regularly now she was no longer working, and he'd wait a few days in the hope that she would eventually reply.

He waited a whole week and then decided he must find out if she was still okay, and so he called round early one evening after work, making sure that her car wasn't parked outside which meant that Joe was out. She seemed delighted to see him when she opened the door.

"Peter, oh, what a lovely surprise! Do come in...Joe isn't here, so..."

They had a coffee and made small talk awhile, both a little hesitant to enter into anything more serious. But then Peter asked her why she hadn't replied to his e-mail, which he'd sent just after their last meeting.

"Oh, I am sorry," she told him. "But I'm afraid I seem to have lost my laptop, so I can't check anything anymore...I just don't know where it's gone...I asked Joe, but he said he doesn't know either..."

Peter guessed right away where it had most likely gone, as Joe had been making things 'disappear' from her office ever since he'd moved in with her, as she'd explained when they last met. It made him cringe with anger, but he controlled his feelings. He hadn't come to upset her, on the contrary.

"Well, it wasn't important," he told her. "Just telling you how much I'd enjoyed seeing you again and the evening out we shared...and if you'd like to do it again sometime..."

"That is nice, Peter. And of course I would, as I told you..."

"Okay, so why not right away?" he chuckled, meaning it.

She looked at him in surprise a moment, then smiled.

"Why not indeed..." she laughed back. "Let me get my glad rags on and we can be off right away..."

They went to a different restaurant, still empty in the early evening, and shared a nice meal. Again, by mutual agreement they didn't order any wine, drinking sparkling water and fruit juice. Carol respected Peter for that. It was totally different from when she went out with Joe, although that hadn't happened for some time now. He was increasingly absent as the time passed, although that didn't upset her anymore. On the contrary.

Peter asked her how things were at home with Joe and all that, and she explained that she hardly saw him now, he was out most of the time running around with his shady business affairs, and he actually told her several times that he didn't enjoy staying in with her now as she was so miserable and sulky and refused to join him in the fun he'd always procured for her. That meant she wouldn't drink with him, nor take the drugs he often insisted she took. Peter sympathised with her, understanding what she must be living through. That decided him even more to come to her aid.

"It's a good thing you're refusing to take part in all that now," he told her." I was really worried when you told me about it last time, and so I really would like to help you, if you'll let me, Carol."

"But I don't see how," she replied. "I mean, not while he's still hanging around all the time…"

"Well, I've spoken to a few people I know, and they run a kind of help service for people in difficulty with drink or drugs, and I could take you to meet them if you want. They're very good and understanding, and it would all stay between us, so what do you think."

"I'm not sure, Peter. I did contact a rehabilitation group myself a few weeks ago, but I don't know if I could go through it all on my own…I remember how my poor mother went through all that when I was a kid, and it nearly destroyed our family…"

"But this is different, really. I'd be with you when you went, and it only happens when you want it to, not like in a clinic or hospital…"

"I could try, I suppose," she said, feeling his sincerity. "And my sister told me she'd help as well, so that would be two of you on my side…"

"That's the spirit!" Peter said, taking hold of her hand and squeezing it tenderly. "I really would like to see you back to your old self, you know…"

She stared deeply into his eyes and realised that what he was feeling towards her was probably what he had experienced long before, when they were working together and had been very close at times. But could she really count on him now? Other disappointments hung over her like a black cloud, and it was difficult for her to see any future clearly.

Peter took Carol home and was pleased to see that Joe was still absent. Carol appeared to have come back to life a little, and he knew it was thanks to him and his caring advice. She wanted him to stay, he knew, but he told her that he had a lot to do with his work for the next day, so he'd better not. And he really didn't want to face Joe again if ever he turned up. So, he left, telling her that he'd arrange a date with the people he knew as soon as he could, and he would accompany her as much as she wanted. They could also go out together anytime she wanted, as he'd really enjoyed that evening with her.

As he left her on the doorstep, he kissed her briefly on the lips, and she felt something she hadn't felt in a very long time. She hardly dared to hope for anything in that direction though, having been disappointed so many times in the past. But it touched her deeply, as when he'd held her hand in the restaurant, and she slept deeply and serenely that night for the first time in ages, dreaming of Peter. Could he be the solution she'd been seeking and hoping for?

Chapter 35

Things started moving rapidly for Carol over the following days and weeks, and she became a lot more confident in herself, trusting those around her who sincerely wished to help her find her former self. Peter introduced her to the people who ran the rehab group, and she was integrated into their system and courses right away. She found it difficult to begin with but soon adapted to it all and was feeling a lot better in herself after just a few sessions.

Elizabeth also came regularly to visit her now, accompanying her when she could to her sessions with therapists and medical staff, encouraging her as best she could to see it through until she was completely cured and free of all toxic influences. That also included Joe, although he wasn't named as such. Carol understood, though, that she must also escape the web of his bad influence if she really wanted to get her life back on track.

She soon felt a lot better in herself now she was no longer drinking or taking drugs of any kind, and she wanted to continue along that road until she became her old self again, as Peter and Elizabeth encouraged her. She could achieve it all, if she really wanted to. Everyone around her told her the same thing, and she started to believe it in herself after a time.

The only blight remained Joe's presence in her life, and even though she hardly saw him now and their relationship had all but ended, he still turned up like a bad penny now and again to use her house, asking her to launder his clothes and feed him and advance some more money so he could get his work done, and assuring her that his big payday was very close now.

She allowed herself to be convinced – and used – every time, much to the annoyance of those close to her, who weren't in the slightest duped about Joe's intentions, although they couldn't impose their will upon her. It had to be her decision, and both Peter and Elizabeth had made that clear to her.

"I'm working on it," she'd tell them with a frown. "I just need more time…"

And so, things advanced slowly, at least on the home front. Joe didn't bother talking with Carol unless it was to ask for something. He never asked how she was or how she was spending her time, and so he knew nothing about her detox sessions, which she kept secret, as that would have enraged him and set things off again. She even wondered sometimes if he'd perhaps met someone else with whom he might be meeting on the quiet, but she dismissed that idea as too far-fetched. No-one in their right mind would hitch up with such a man now, she felt certain, and all his so-called friends were just part of the drug gang he had joined just after moving in with her.

He appeared to have totally lost interest in her now, never showed her any affection, and when he did come home and crash into her bed in the early hours of the morning, there was never any show of affection between them, even when Carol attempted to take the initiative.

He no longer tried to induce her to take drugs either, but that side of it pleased her. She wanted that to be over, if not the rest. He remained indifferent, nonetheless. She knew he was getting deeply involved with things that most likely were far above his reach and talent, but he never asked her for advice, nor even talked about what he was doing. She'd become the outsider, and he used her as a stopping-off place when he needed cleaning up and to recuperate a bit. Then he'd ask her for money, take her car, and she wouldn't see him again for days on end, returning when he needed help again. She saw it for what it was but remained as a slave to his needs, nonetheless. That was how she was made, she told herself as an excuse. But it was wearing thin, even inside her own thoughts.

Then one evening Joe came home looking very nervous and jittery, and Carol saw at once that he wasn't his usual uncaring self for once. He was carrying a large holdall, which he kept close to him all the time, and this again roused Carol's suspicions.

"Has something happened, Joe?" she asked him in a concerned tone, really wanting to help him if she could.

He looked at her as if just noticing his presence.

"It's better you don't know anything about it," he replied bluntly. "What you don't know can't hurt you, so..."

"Well, I'm here to help if I can," she told him. "I know we haven't been getting on lately, but I still love you, Joe, and I want things to go back to how they were when we first met again..."

"Ha, fat chance of that ever happening now!" he scowled.

"But won't you tell me what's wrong?" she insisted. "I will help if I can..."

"Ah, Carol, I think I'm beyond help right now, to be honest. I've been accused of things they won't forgive, believe you me, and if I don't sort it out now God knows what will happen…"

"You mean your bosses?"

"Exactly…they called me in and accused me of all kinds of things, and if I can't prove otherwise, well, enough to say they won't treat me as a friend any longer…"

"Oh, Joe, I am sorry…"

"Me too…but sorry won't fix things with them. Anyway, I'm going to bed now to try and sleep a bit, because I'll have to leave very early tomorrow…so if anyone knocks on the door, don't open it whatever you do…"

He went upstairs then, still carrying the holdall, leaving Carol in a distressed sate of alarm. She put two and two together and guessed they'd found out about his cheating them, whoever they were, and she was world-wise enough to know that in such cases there was never any leeway or forgiveness.

After a while she decided to call Peter, as she couldn't settle and didn't know what to do for the best.

"Sorry to bother you so late," she said, talking softly so as not to alert Joe.

"Are you all right, Carol? Is something wrong?"

"It's Joe," she told him. "I think he's in trouble with the people he deals with, and he thinks they'll be coming after him soon…"

"Oh, no, that's something you can do without right now. Do you want me to come over?"

"No, not now, he's gone to bed, and he said he'll leave early in the morning. But if you could call round tomorrow that would be good..."

"All right, I will, no problem. But if anything happens, don't hesitate to call me, will you? I can be there quickly..."

"All right, I will...and thanks, Peter. I needed to hear a true friend's voice..."

"Well, you know I'll always be here for you..."

"I know...and I'm so glad..."

She sat on a bit, confused and frightened, but no-one came to the door, and she eventually went up to bed, where she found Joe curled up like a baby, fully dressed, and with his arm firmly gripped around the holdall. She couldn't think straight any longer and eventually fell asleep under a dark cloud of worry.

When she awoke the following morning, she was alone. Joe had gone. She hadn't heard a thing, so he must have left very early, as he'd told her he would, and without making a noise. She still felt worried yet also relieved in way. She looked out from the bedroom window to check if he'd taken her car. He had. That bothered her a little, as she had no idea now where he'd gone and when he would be back. All this with her car, which was still registered in her name, as was the tax and insurance.

Peter arrived just after breakfast and looked relieved to find Carol on her own and seemingly all right. He had himself spent a restless night worrying about her. Carol made some coffee, and they sat in the kitchen discussing the situation. Carol wanted and needed a lasting solution to this problem, and Peter wanted her to be permanently free from such worries. But how to achieve this without too much upheaval and damage?

"I think he's stolen from them," she told him then, wanting him to be an ally. "And so now they want their money and goods back, and I think he's done a runner…"

"Well, that might not be a bad thing," Peter replied. "I mean, if he can't safely come back here you might not see him again in a while…"

"Yes, I know that. But he's taken my car, and that might implicate me in the whole situation, as well as the fact that he was living in my house for so long. I was wondering if I should go to the police and tell them the whole story…"

"Hm, well, I wouldn't do that if I were you," Peter said, looking a bit startled. "I think it better to wait a while and see what unfolds…he might well be back in a day or two and then you could judge the situation a lot better. And if you did talk to the police and he hears about it that might set him against you as well…"

"Yes, maybe you're right. But I do want my car back, and I don't see why he has the right just to go off and leave me like this all the time. Now, with those people after him it makes me feel worse, but he doesn't care, of course."

"Well, just try to be patient, Carol. I'll be around if you need me, so let's wait a few days and see how things advance…"

"Yes, I think you're right…it's just being alone here with all that hanging over me that makes me so nervous…even scared…what if they do come here looking for him? What do I do then?"

"Just tell them he isn't here, and you don't know where he is. I don't think they'd harm you at all, because that would upset their own things even more and such people like to stay under the radar. But I could come and stay here with you if you wanted, just to be sure…"

"Oh, Peter, thank you, but I don't want to derange you in your life, really. I'll be okay, I'm sure…"

"Well, the offer stands, if you need me. Don't forget."

"I won't…and thank you so much…"

"I do care about you, Carol, really I do…"

"I know…and I'm glad. That makes me feel safe…"

"Good. I'm sure it will all sort itself out eventually, so try not to worry…"

He put his arms around her, and she rested her head on his chest. He didn't want to leave her in this condition, but he needed to go to work.

"I have to go now," he told her. "Important business meeting. But I'll call you this evening to see how you are, and you can call me anytime, remember…"

"You're so good to me, Peter," she told him then. "Always there for me when I need some support. Will you promise to always be my friend?"

"Of course I will. I think that in a different life, things would have turned out so differently for both of us..."

He left her then, driving away and wondering in himself if that different life could still become a reality for them. He knew deep down that this was what he wanted now, more than anything else. As for Carol, his words bore deep into her soul as she sat and pondered over them. What did he mean? Was there a chance that he still found her attractive and worthy of his deepest affection. She felt a slight flicker of hope, and that was enough at that time.

Feeling a little better, she decided to call Elizabeth and tell her about what was happening. She still came regularly to visit, but now Carol was over the worst with her drug and alcohol addictions, they had seen less of each other. Elizabeth also had her own family to take care of.

"Do you think he's gone for good then?" she asked when Carol had explained the situation.

"I don't know. He looked really worried, and he wasn't his normal self. I just don't know what to do for the best right now."

"Well, there isn't a lot you can do I suppose, apart from wait to see if he comes back."

"That's what Peter said as well..."

Elizabeth felt relieved that Peter was closer to her than she was, and she knew how much he doted upon her, having been with them both a lot during her therapy sessions. She much preferred him over Joe, but of course, it was Carol who needed to make decisions, not her. She could advise, but not much more.

"Well, if you need me to come up and stay with you a bit, let me know, won't you? And you can always come to us if you want, you know that."

"Thank you, Elizabeth. I'm so happy to have you back in my life, I really am. I don't know what would have happened if I hadn't listened to you and to Peter, you know…"

"I know…I can't make decisions for you, I know that, but you'd have been much better off staying with Peter instead of falling in with that Joe again…he was never really interested in anyone but himself, even at the home…but you must make your own choices, of course, as I did when I met Sid and gave up my life in the convent…"

"You're right, and I do agree with you. But I do worry about Joe, and I do love him still…I just hope he's all right, wherever he is…"

"Well, wait a couple of days and see if he turns up. And stay in touch with me, whatever happens. You can count on my help, you know that."

"Thank you…I will…"

For the rest of that day she lingered at home, waiting for some sign of life from Joe, a call or perhaps a visit, but nothing happened. Peter called her in the evening for an update, and she told him that nothing had happened, and she was feeling okay. She spent another troubled night, but managed to sleep a little, thanking her blessings that Peter and her sister were with her, at least in thought. The rest would happen as it did, and she would have to accept it. That was what destiny was about, and she was learning fast.

Chapter 36

For the next three days she sat and waited at home in a state of half-awareness, torn between a craving for Joe's return and half-hoping he was gone for good. That induced feelings of culpability, but she understood now where her own best interests lay, and Joe didn't feature.

She went constantly to the front window and stared out fixedly, wanting her car to pull up outside, but it didn't. Each time she heard a car engine approaching she would rush over and look out, always in vain. She was truly worried by now in case something bad had happened to Joe which stopped him returning, and her thoughts turned again towards going to the police and reporting him missing. But again, she feared that this might open a whole can of worms she wouldn't be able to handle, as Peter had warned her, and so she hesitated, waiting for any sign that might bring relief, no matter how small.

Both Peter and Elizabeth had called every day to find out if there was any news, and she told them that she'd heard nothing and was still worried. They both offered to visit her, but she told them she preferred to stay alone just in case Joe did turn up. She was okay and would let them know as soon as there was any news. Inside, she would have loved to have them both with her as a kind of lifebelt and security, but she didn't want to derange them any further, as she knew they both had their own lives and problems to tend to each day, and it wasn't fair to ask them constantly for aid. She was the only one responsible for her situation, and she knew that now very well.

She called Peter again later that evening, unable to bear the stress and tension any longer. She really needed to see somebody, and preferably that would be him. He guessed from her tone of voice that she wasn't feeling too good.

"Are you all right, Carol?" he asked. "Has something happened?"

"No, everything's just the same, no news of Joe at all, but I'm just worried that something bad might have happened to him. It's been three days now and I don't know what to do for the best...I'm just pacing up and down all the time and can't stop fretting..."

"Would you like me to pop round?" he asked, concerned.

"Oh, that would be lovely if you could...but I don't want to bother you..."

"It's no bother, really...I was just thinking about you anyway, and I'd love to see you again, so..."

"Thank you, Peter..."

"Okay, I'll be there in a jiffy..."

She felt a great comfort as Peter walked in and embraced her warmly, kissing her softly on the cheek. He was casually but smartly dressed as always, and he gave off an enticing scent that rekindled past moments she'd spent in his arms, before the advent of Joe in her life had upset the balance and drove this kind man away. But she knew that regrets solved nothing. He was there with her again now, and for that she was thankful. The future would play itself out no matter what her feelings, and she had at least learnt that now as she sat waiting for news of Joe.

They sat together in the living room and drank tea. Peter was pained to see her in this state and thought hard about what he could do to help her once and for all. Inside, he knew full well what he wanted but felt he couldn't impose his desires onto her until all this business had been cleared away. He sat listening to her and comforted her as best he could with reassuring words. She appeared to relax a little then.

"Do you think I should report him missing tomorrow morning?" she asked then.

"I don't know. If you do, at least you'll know that they'll be looking for him, and that would be for his own good as well as your peace of mind. But as I told you before, it will mean lots of questions about you and Joe, and I'm not sure you'll be able to face all that…"

"But I have to do something, Peter. I can't just sit here every day and worry myself sick about him…you do understand that, don't you?"

"Yes, of course I do…I just want you to understand what might be involved…"

"I think I'll deal with that if and when I have to…as long as you and Elizabeth are on my side, I'm sure I'll get through it okay…"

"All right then, I'll come with you tomorrow if you want, and we'll just tell them that he's disappeared with your car and you're worried about him…they'll take it from there, I think…"

"Thank you, Peter. I have to set my mind at rest, you understand?"

"Of course I do, don't worry. I want you to be free from all this hassle anyway, and then maybe you can get your life back on track again…"

She stared hard at him again for a moment, as though scrutinising him and trying to discover his true intentions towards her. She still felt highly attracted to him, certain that if Joe hadn't turned up that evening she would have stayed with him despite their differences at the time. But no regrets, she told herself again.

"Thank you," she murmured again, taking his hand and squeezing it tenderly. "I'm so happy to have you near me again, you know…"

"Well, the feeling's mutual, you know, so…"

They sat huddled together for some time, simply enjoying that chaste togetherness. They both needed it at that moment, perhaps for different reasons, but just as strongly in each of them. It felt as though time had stopped, and they were caught in a warp of their own making. But it passed, and they came back down to earth with a sigh.

"Do you want to stay the night?" Carol asked, not pleading but perhaps hoping a little.

"I'd better not," Peter told her with a hint of regret. "If he came back in the middle of the night and found me here…well, you know what I mean, don't you?"

"Yes, of course, don't worry. You're quite right, I know…"

"Let's wait and see what happens first," Peter went on. "And tomorrow I'll go with you to the police station and let them take things in hand. Okay?"

"Yes, okay. I think we must do that now anyway. And thanks for all your help, and comforting…"

"My pleasure…" he told her, kissing her gently on the forehead.

He left shortly afterwards, with his own thoughts in a whirlwind of doubts and possibilities. But he was certain of one thing: she felt for him what he had always felt for her, and that kept him determined to do the right thing by her, whatever. She deserved better now for the remainder of her life, and he would see that it happened, if he could.

Carol suffered similar thoughts, but on a different level. Peter was a rock. Joe was a swamp. She had to decide which she wanted to walk upon.

Chapter 37

The following day, Peter came to pick up Carol and drove her to the local police station. She was feeling a lot calmer than she'd imagined she would, as if this was a first step towards putting things right. She also felt a great comfort in Peter's presence, as he tended to remain calm in whatever the circumstances, as she'd noticed before.

It was all very matter of fact that first time, with an officer taking a statement from Carol as though it were something he did every day. Because Joe was not a minor nor a person in danger, there was no priority given to his disappearance, and as the officer explained calmly, in 99% of such cases the person involved often turned up after a week or so. But he recorded all the details, including the fact that he'd taken off in Carol's car, which was immediately signalled to the traffic department, who could then watch out for it. And that was it, much to Carol's surprise and relief.

"Thank you for coming with me," she said to Peter as he drove her home.

"My pleasure," he replied.

"But don't you think it all seemed a bit too straight forward," she continued. "I mean, apart from a few personal questions about us living together, they didn't seem too interested in Joe and his lifestyle, did they?

"Well, that's perhaps a good thing," Peter told her. "The less they know the better, I think..."

"Yes, you're probably right…"

He dropped her off and returned to work, telling her he'd contact her that evening, unless she called him first with any news.

"Keep your spirits up," he told her before driving away. "You've done the right thing now so let's just wait and see what happens, eh?"

"Yes, all right. And thanks again…"

Alone again, she called Elizabeth, wanting to keep her up to date and to hear her voice. She explained what had happened at the police station, and that now she just had to wait for them to do their job, although Joe was one among many, as the police officer had informed her, and he wasn't top priority. But it seemed to calm Elizabeth's nerves, as she'd been worried about what might happen if the police looked more closely at Joe's way of life. She agreed with Carol that all they could do now was wait, and hope, and in her case, pray for a happy ending. Carol appreciated that thought. She admired Elizabeth for her unbending faith and devotion and sometimes wished she could be the same. But she knew that was impossible now; she had travelled too far the other way down the dark roads that seemed to lead to only one goal, and which no longer appealed to her. She had learnt her lesson, she told Elizabeth, and she wouldn't fall again if she could help it. Elizabeth sensed that determination in her voice and told her to stay on this new route to happiness.

"I will, Elizabeth, I promise…"

"Good. And I'll come to see you again soon, but let me know if you hear anything, won't you?"

"Yes, of course…and thank you for being there for me…"

The very next day there was some news, although it was difficult for Carol to decide whether it was good or bad. Before noon there was a knock at her door, and she opened it to find two police officers in uniform standing before her. They asked if they could come in and talk with her. She dreaded the worst as she invited them in.

"Is there some news?" she asked, obviously worried.

"We've come to let you know that we've located your car," they told her then.

"Oh…where was it?" she asked, a little confused and relieved together.

"In the car park of the Red Lion pub…"

"Ah…and is there any sign of Joe at all? I mean…"

"No, just the car, parked and locked. We wondered if you have a spare key we could have, as we need to examine it before you can take it back…"

"Oh, yes, of course…I'll get it…"

She handed over her key and they thanked her and made to leave.

"Have you any idea where Joe might be?" she asked then, anxious for any news.

"No, not at the moment, I'm afraid. But C.I.D. officers are on the case now, and they discovered that Joe was a regular at that pub, so they are continuing their enquiries…"

"That's good then. I mean, if the car was there that means he's probably not far away, doesn't it?"

"I'm afraid we can't tell you anything yet…but don't worry, they'll find him no doubt once all the facts are a bit clearer…and we'll let you know when you can collect your car, probably in a day or two…"

"Okay, thank you…"

When they left, she immediately called Peter to let him know the news.

"Well, that's something," he told her. "At least you'll get your car back…"

"Yes, but why would they want to keep it?" she asked naively.

"Oh, that's routine I should imagine, looking for any clues of where he might have gone or what's happened to him. Don't worry, I'm sure they'll find him soon enough now…"

"I do hope so," Carol sighed. "This is all really getting on top of me again, I'm afraid…"

"Well, try to stay strong, for me…" he told her. "We'll get through this if we stick together, I promise…and if you like, I'll pop round after work this evening and we can have a chat about things…"

"That would be nice…thanks…"

She felt relieved after speaking with Peter and felt a warmth inside which she hadn't felt lately with Joe. She brushed it aside however and decided to call Elizabeth and let her know of the developments. Like Peter, she was glad to hear that things were moving, no matter how slowly. She also told Carol to keep her informed, and that she would come to see her if the need arose. Thus comforted, Carol settled down to another long day of waiting.

It was turning into a way of life, and she wanted badly to break out of it but wasn't sure how she could do that. 'Wait and see what happens' had become almost a way of life, but she felt she could see light at the end of the tunnel again. She prayed that it would hurry to reach her.

Peter dropped by as planned after work and found Carol in quite a state, much to his surprise. He wondered if there had been any more news from the police concerning Joe.

"No, it's just that I've been sitting here all day imaging all sorts of horrible things and it's made me feel a bit depressed..."

"I'm sorry to hear that," Peter told her, concerned for her well-being. "You should have called me, and I'd have come straight over..."

"But I can't keep deranging you," she replied. "I've made this mess and it's up to me to get out of it..."

"Well, that's true in some respects, but it's not all your fault, after all you've been through...I do understand that, you know."

She looked at him with that solemn stare again, as if trying to gauge his sincerity. She saw that he meant it and felt warm inside again. How had she ever chosen to be with Joe instead of this man, she asked herself again.

"Thanks for telling me that," she said. "You do mean such a lot to me now, really..."

"I'm glad to hear it..."

They spent a quiet evening together, with Carol rustling-up a make-do dinner for Peter while trying not to think about Joe and the many problems he'd caused her. She had lost her own appetite since these troubles began, but Peter insisted she eat a little with him.

"You have to look after yourself," he told her. "Don't let yourself go again, will you?"

"No, don't worry, I won't...I just need this to be over and then I'll be all right, I'm sure. I feel much better generally anyway since you and Elizabeth have been helping me and since I stopped drinking and all that again..."

"Good, that's nice to know...just make sure you keep it up, won't you...for me..."

"Yes, don't worry, I will...

He left shortly after eating, as they both thought there would be no news that night and he preferred to go home and keep his affairs in order with his business. She understood, recalling how quickly her own affairs had floundered when Joe came along and threw her attention off-balance. Peter told her he'd call first thing and then they could take things from there. He was available whenever she might need help or company, and he insisted on that. She kissed him softly as he left and then managed to get through the night relatively peacefully on her own. Tomorrow was another day, she told herself. She would face it then when it came.

Chapter 38

Things remained quiet over the following days, and although Carol called the police station regularly the response was always the same: we are still following our enquiries, and as soon as we know anything we will contact you. She resigned herself to this waiting game.

Then one evening as she sat talking with Peter, there came a loud knock at the front door, and she rushed to open it to find a woman police officer in uniform and a man in plain clothes, both looking rather grim. Her heart missed a beat, and she felt that she knew what they were going to say.

"Miss Carol Williams?" the man asked.

"Yes…"

"I'm Detective-Inspector John Draycot, and this is W.P.C. Leslie Billingham," the man told her as they both displayed their warrant cards. "May we come in? I'm afraid we have some rather bad news for you…"

Peter had followed Carol to the door, and now he put his arm around her shoulders as she let out a soft moan. He had also guessed what that news would likely be.

"Do come in," he told the police officers as he made way for them, leading Carol back into the living room.

"Thank you," the man replied. "And you are?"

"Peter Tierney…I'm a close friend of Carol…"

They went into the living room, where Carol and Peter sat on the sofa and the police officers in the armchairs. The atmosphere was suddenly very intense.

"Have you found Joe?" Carol managed to ask in a strained voice.

"We think so," the detective replied. "We have discovered a man's body that fits his description, and we would like you to come to the mortuary to identify the body, if you would…"

Carol just stared in disbelief at the man, her face chalk-white, her thoughts in total chaos. Had she heard him correctly, she wondered. Surely, they would know if it was Joe's body they had found; they had the photo she'd provided, so why would she have to go and look at him and identify him. Was she losing her sanity, or what? Peter took her hand and squeezed it softly, to let her know that he was still there with her.

"Do I have to?" she asked the detective.

"No, if you prefer not to that's your prerogative, of course. But it would really help us to be certain, and as you were the person closest to him at the time of his disappearance, and since he has no family as far as we are aware, you are the only one we know who could give us a positive identification."

She looked from his face to Peter's, trying to make sense of all this while breaking into pieces deep inside. Joe was dead, that was what the man was telling her. Dead. A body lying in the mortuary. And they needed her to go and identify that body. Her beloved Joe. The crazy boy she'd met as a child and who'd led her a merry dance over the last few months, now lying cold and still on a slab at the local mortuary. Could it possibly be real? She released a howl of sheer agony then that caused those present to jump a little, while Peter hugged her close to him, knowing everything he might do now would be inadequate.

"Can we leave it until tomorrow?" Peter asked the detective, for whom this was, of course, just one more delicate part of his job.

"Yes, of course," he replied, having lived through this countless times. "I didn't expect her to go this evening. What time would suit you best?"

"Late morning, I think," Peter told him, as Carol sat and sobbed uncontrollably beside him. "I'll accompany her, if that's all right..."

"Yes, certainly, of course...and I am so sorry to have to bring this news to her like this, but we have to know, you understand..."

"Yes, of course...don't worry, I'll stay with her now and make sure she's all right."

"That's good. She shouldn't be left alone right now. Shall we say 11 o'clock, then tomorrow?"

"Yes, all right...I'll make sure she gets there..."

"You know where the mortuary is, at the local hospital?"

"Yes, I'll find it, don't worry."

"Good. I'll be waiting for you at the reception, anyway. And we'll also need to talk with her sometime soon about Joe and his life, and take a statement from her, so she might want to contact a lawyer..."

"Really? You don't think she's involved, do you?"

"We know very little right now, as it's still under investigation. But as she is the only person we know who was in contact with him, it's normal that we need to question her and find out about his lifestyle and the people he frequented, that's all."

"Okay, I'll talk with her when she's calmed down...can I ask what happened? I mean, to the body you found..."

"He was shot, I'm afraid, so it is a murder investigation, but I'd ask you to keep that information to yourselves until we have completed our enquiries..."

"Yes, of course..."

"We'll see you tomorrow morning then. Good night, sir..."

"Er, yes, good night, detective..."

He locked the door after them and went back to Carol, who was still sobbing her heart out on the sofa. He sat close beside her and comforted her as best he could in silence, letting her sob her way to relief. He knew what she must be going through, and he was excluded for the time being.

"I'll make some tea," he said as her sobbing became a faint wailing. "It'll do you good..."

Carol was calm when he brought the tea in. He saw that as a good sign.

"Are you okay?" he asked anyway, lost for words himself right then.

"I don't think I'll ever be okay," she blubbered. "Things just seem to keep happening to me every time I think I've found happiness, and it's been going on ever since I was a kid, I think...what have I done to deserve this now?"

"I don't know, Carol, to be honest. I think it's just bad luck that you bumped into Joe that night at the pub, and so you're not to blame really, nor anyone else. It's just destiny that comes along and shakes us up and we're pretty much helpless to fight back against it..."

"Do you really believe that?"

"Sometimes I do, yes. The same as when we met, and we both had troubles of our own that separated us as well, if you remember. Now Joe has brought us back together, so that might well be another strike of destiny for all we know..."

"So, we're all helpless then if that's the way it is..."

"Yes, it would seem so..."

They sat in silence, drinking the tea and pondering on all that had happened that evening and all that had been said. Carol slowly gathered her spirits together and was so glad that Peter had been with her during the police visit. Alone she would have collapsed, she knew, or even worse.

"Did they say how he died?" she asked then, as if that question had been irrelevant before.

"He was shot, or so the detective told me..."

She stared incredulously at him, not wanting to hear, not wanting to know, not wanting to believe. But now she did.

"Oh my God...poor Joe...so they obviously found him then..."

"It looks that way, yes. It's a murder investigation anyway, and they want you to make a statement when you feel ready..."

"Me? Why me? Do they think I'm mixed up with all that?"

"No, I don't think so. It's just that he'd been living here with you and had your car, so they need to get your version of the facts and eliminate you from their enquiries. They probably know who it was anyway, so you needn't worry about that."

"As long as they don't come looking for me as well now to make sure I don't talk to the police...they're a nasty bunch, that's for sure. We can see that now after what they've done to Joe..."

"That's true. You might be better coming to stay at my place for tonight, at least until we find out more about it all tomorrow. What do you think?"

"You wouldn't mind?"

"Of course not... I'd rather it were in different circumstances, but, seriously, I think you'd feel safer and more comfortable."

"Okay... and thanks. I don't know what I'd do without you, really, I don't."

"Well, I'm glad I was around to be able to help."

"I'd better call Elizabeth and let her know...she's worried about me as well..."

"Okay. Then grab what you need, and we'll go to my place. We've got to be at the mortuary tomorrow morning at eleven..."

"Oh, dear God…I'm not sure I'll be able to handle that, really…"

"Don't worry, I'll be with you…"

She looked deeply into his eyes again and saw the love that he was overflowing with at that very instant. Again, she asked herself if she hadn't been too hasty in ditching him for Joe, although that quickly passed. She had to stay practical now, she knew. All this was far from over.

She packed a small night bag, and they left her home to drive to Peter's. It would be a long and terrible night for her, she knew that already, and she could feel Joe knocking at the door of her soul even as they drove through the dark streets. She was happy when Peter left her alone in his spare bedroom, the one his children used when visiting. She needed to be alone, yet knowing that he was near, just in case. It was a fitful night for both of them.

Chapter 39

The identification of Joe's body was another terrible ordeal she had to face. Peter drove her to the hospital, where they found D.I. Draycot waiting for them by the reception. He greeted them cordially but firmly, and asked them to accompany him to the mortuary, where they entered the forensic section. This was where the forensic team worked with the police to seek clues and solve crimes, as much as they were able. It looked to be a grim sort of place to Carol as they walked in, and the odour hanging in the air reminded her of hospitals and operating theatres. She shuddered a little and braced herself as best she could.

A trolley was wheeled in, covered with a green plastic sheet.

"Are you ready?" the detective asked.

Carol nodded her head, while Peter held her arm and tried to be strong enough for them both. This wasn't easy for her, as he well knew. The mortician pulled back the sheet a little to reveal Joe's face, and Carol let out a short cry as she looked at the lifeless head, which resembled a waxwork more than a living visage. It was no longer the happy-go-lucky Joe she'd co-habited with over the past months.

"Can you confirm that this is Joseph Fowler?" the detective asked her, wanting this to be over as quickly as she did.

"Yes…" Carol replied, her voice breaking into sobs. "It is my Joe…"

"Thank you," the detective replied, nodding at the mortician, who re-covered the face and then wheeled the body away back to the cold storage room.

Carol had buried her face into Peter's chest, sobbing silently as he tried to comfort her, although he knew full well that she was beyond any comfort at that moment. This was another of life's senseless lessons, and those involved had to simply accept the facts and then try to get on with their own lives as best they could. Simple in theory, but so very difficult when it happened to you or someone close to you. And no words can ever make things better, as he knew from experience. Carol also knew, of course, having lost both her parents; and now the loss of Joe was a raw wound she felt would never heal.

"We still need you to come into the station and answer a few questions," the detective then told her. "When it's convenient, of course."

"Yes, I understand," Carol manage to say. "Not today though, I hope...?"

"No, of course not, only when you feel you're ready...but the sooner we know all about your life with Joe and his routines, the better for us. We need to find the people who did this and get them off the streets and locked away for a long time. I'm sure you understand that..."

"Yes, I understand...what about tomorrow?"

"If you're sure..."

"I am. I want to get all this over with and get my old life back as soon as I can, so I'll come tomorrow and answer your questions."

"And I'll accompany her again, if that's allowed?" Peter added.

"Yes, of course. What time would suit you best, both of you?"

Carol looked hard at Peter in a pleading manner, and he understood that she wanted him to be in charge right now, as she was still floundering inside with confusion and grief. He squeezed her hand again and smiled at her.

"Shall we say 2 o'clock?" he said to the detective.

"Fine, that will be okay. I'll be waiting at the station…"

"Will we need to bring a lawyer?" Peter then asked, a little anxious still.

"No, not tomorrow, unless you feel the need. It will just be to answer a few questions to let me get a clearer picture of Joe's character and how he operated. Later, if I need a formal statement, we can talk about lawyers and all that, if that's okay with you?"

"Yes, that's fine," Carol told him. "I really do want to move on…"

They left the hospital then, and Peter drove Carol back home. She was silent during the whole voyage, and he respected that need. He could only imagine what she was going through in her thoughts, and it pained him to be on the outside all of that again. He still had a vague hope buried deep inside that now, perhaps, she would let him in again eventually, but he knew it would take time for her to assimilate this whole drama and then recover from it, if ever she could.

Arriving at the house, they were both surprised to find Elizabeth's car parked outside. As they pulled up, Elizabeth got out of her car and came to greet them.

"Oh, my poor dear," she murmured as Carol fell into her arms. "This is all so dreadful. How are you?"

"I'm okay," Carol told her. I just need to rest and think about everything for a while...it *was* Joe they found, you see..."

"Oh, no...I'm so sorry..."

She looked at Peter, who shrugged his shoulders and nodded at her. She understood.

"Well, I hope you don't mind my turning up like this...I just couldn't wait any longer not knowing what was happening..."

"No, it's all right, don't worry...I'm really pleased to see you."

"Let's go inside and I'll make some tea," Peter said. "I think we all could all use a cuppa right now..."

"Thank you," Carol said, looking at him in that strange way once again.

They moved inside, feeling glad to be together but also wondering about what was going to happen next and how this whole drama would play out. A difficult time for all of them.

Elizabeth had a lot of questions she wanted to ask, of course, but she knew it best to remain silent until Carol opened up a bit, or not, accordingly. They sipped their tea and made small talk for a while, with Carol obviously struggling to remain lucid under the pressure of what she had learned so far about Joe. How could she have been so blind? They do say that love is blind, but now she felt almost certain that it was.

"So, what happens now?" Elizabeth asked eventually, unable to contain her own feelings.

"I'm going to talk to the police tomorrow," Carol told her.

"Oh?"

"Yes," Peter joined in. "They need Carol to tell them some details about Joe's life while he was living here with her…it is a murder investigation now, you see…"

"Oh, how dreadful…" Elizabeth uttered, upset. "Are they sure about that?"

"Yes," Carol told her softly. "He was shot…"

A new silence descended over them then as Elizabeth digested this news. She had never really got on with Joe, even as children, and now she saw clearly that he had caused such a lot of damage to Carol, first with drink and drugs, and now with this sordid tale of dealers and gangsters. She found it difficult to grasp right away.

"Oh, poor Joe…" she muttered. "He didn't deserve that, I'm sure…"

"No, he didn't," Carol agreed. "He just didn't get a real chance in life, even as a kid…we both know that…"

"Well, you were all in the same boat as I understand it," Peter joined in. "And you seem to have come through all right..."

"Chance," Carol cried emphatically. "It's all about chance, I think. Like it was just chance that I bumped into him again...if I hadn't, who knows what would have happened to him..."

"But you mustn't blame yourself, Carol," Elizabeth said firmly. "None of it is your fault...on the contrary, I'm sure you tried your best to help him..."

"That's true," Peter added. "I saw that with my own eyes..."

"Well, we can't change anything now," Carol admitted. "What's done is done, and I'll just have to learn to live with it."

"Of course," Elizabeth agreed. "None of us can fight against our destiny really, we have to accept it all as it happens..."

"Well, I think I'll go and lie down a bit if you don't mind," Carol said. "I need to be alone and try to rest..."

"Of course, don't worry," Peter told her. "We're here for you now, whatever..."

Peter told Elizabeth he would have to leave shortly and go back to work, and so Elizabeth told him that she'd stay with Carol, and not to worry. She wouldn't leave her on her own.

"Good," Peter said. "You know I have been worrying about her a lot lately, and now this has happened it's worse..."

"It's a good thing you are around when she needs you," Elizabeth told him. "I think she depends on you now, and I know you have feelings for her..."

"Is it that so obvious?" he chuckled, amused.

"Perhaps because we're sisters and we know each other pretty well…it's not a bad thing though, I'm sure of that…"

"I hope you're right. To be honest, I'm glad that Joe is out of her life now, although I wouldn't have wished this on him…"

"I understand, and I agree. I never really liked him, even when we were kids…"

"Well, I'm glad you're here, anyway, and I'll call by this evening after work, tell Carol. And if you want to go back home then I'll watch over her…"

"Okay, let's see how she is later on…"

Peter left, and Elizabeth settled down to wait. Carol was silent, and when Elizabeth went up and peeked into her bedroom, she found her fast asleep, no doubt from sheer exhaustion.

"Ah, my poor Carol," she murmured softly. "You really didn't deserve this, I know…"

It was a long afternoon for her then, as she sat and reminisced alone over both their lives.

Chapter 40

Elizabeth stayed at Carol's the following day when she went with Peter to answer questions about her life with Joe. She wanted to know how things stood before returning to her own family. She was happy to see that Carol appeared a lot calmer than on the previous day, although she imagined what she must be going through in her mind.

It was all straightforward to begin with at the police station, simple questions about how Carol and Joe had met, and about her own life after her mother's death. They'd obviously done their homework. She answered as best she could, bravely and honestly. She could feel they were far more interested in what Joe had been doing and with whom, of which Carol knew very little. He'd shut her out from the start, although she did tell them about how he'd introduced her to drug taking, which led to her addiction and consequent rehabilitation.

She had questions of her own, but D.I. Draycot repeated that the investigation was still ongoing, but she would eventually have access to all the information they were gathering. It was a complex case, but he did let on that the police had been watching Joe for quite some time, wanting to discover his contacts, who were the real bad guys. Joe had become involved with some very nasty people, falling into their hands and under their control, and it was vital now that the police got hold of them and put them away for a long time. Carol agreed with most of that.

"He was just a bit naïve, I think," she told the officer. "Easily led and all that...he wasn't a bad person deep down, on the contrary, when we first got together he was really loving and sweet and made me so happy..."

The inspector said nothing. There was a lot he wasn't telling Carol as yet, because he knew that speed was essential in this enquiry, and so he got as much information as he could and then allowed Carol to leave, telling her they would have to talk with her again very soon, and possibly look around her house in case Joe had left any evidence there they might use. She agreed and then went back home with Peter. Elizabeth was still there, anxious for an update.

"They seem more interested in the people Joe was working with than him," Carol told her. "It sounds like they're a really nasty gang of international traffickers, and Joe got on the wrong side of them..."

"But they know you were never involved in any of that, do they?" Elizabeth asked.

"Yes, I'm pretty sure they do...I told them everything, anyway, about Joe and the drugs he made me take and all that, so they do know, I think. They told me it's not the first time this has happened in that kind of set-up, looking for a safe place to stay and hide away in while they're up to their nasty business..."

"Dreadful," Elizabeth commented. "And you thought he was genuine..."

"Yes...I still think he may have been, at least in the beginning, anyway...he just seemed so nice all the time at first..."

"Well, it's over now," Peter said, joining in. "They call it the cuckoo syndrome, I think...moving into someone's nest to lay their eggs...that's what the police told me, anyway..."

"Terrible," Elizabeth shuddered at the thought. "I still think you're well rid of all that now, Carol...really..."

"Yes, probably...but it's still hard to accept...he did have a good side as well, you know..."

Elizabeth and Peter looked at each other with a frown. They both knew better and accepted the truth of the situation. Carol would need time, that was certain. But they both hoped she would pull through and become her happy self again.

Elizabeth left shortly after to return to her family, telling Carol to call whenever she wanted to, or even visit if she felt the need to talk or be with people. And she would come to Carol if ever the need arose. Carol was relieved to hear that. With both Elizabeth and Peter now on her side and available, she felt a new determination and strength inside, and was determined to pull herself through this ordeal, no matter how difficult it proved to be. It was far from over, as she well knew.

Peter stayed on a while, talking with Carol and trying to reassure her about the police and their investigation. He understood far more than she did the ins and outs of their enquiries, and he reassured her once again that she wasn't on their list of suspects or anything else. She'd been used, and that was an end to it. Carol thanked him again for being there for her now, and she felt a new kind of togetherness growing between them, even among the ruins of this terrible tragedy. She still daren't hope for too much though. Not yet.

Chapter 41

Things moved a lot faster when the police came to search Carol's house a few days later. The search was led by D.I. Draycot and several uniformed policemen and women. There was no sense of intimidation or aggression, since the detective knew that Carol hadn't been involved in any of Joe's illegal activities, but they needed to make sure that he hadn't left any vital evidence behind. Carol understood this and sat with Peter in the living room. He'd come round to be with her, knowing she'd be too nervous on her own. The detective sat with them.

The search moved through the whole house, room by room, inspecting all the cupboards and nooks and crannies where he might have stashed something, but none of the officers searching found anything out of the ordinary. Joe had obviously cleared out everything on the day he left, which frustrated the inspector a little, although he had almost expected it.

"Well, it looks like he left nothing that might help us identify his colleagues," he told Carol and Peter. "They are usually clever at getting rid of traces..."

"Was there anything in the car?" Carol asked then. "He did have a big bag with him on the last night he stayed here, and he never let it out of his sight."

"No, the car was empty, so I think they must have taken that bag when they got hold of Joe..."

They were preparing to leave, when one of the policemen came down the stairs holding something in his gloved hand.

"I found this stuffed behind the bathroom cabinet," the policeman announced, handing a small black notebook to the detective.

D.I. Draycot took it and leafed through it, curious.

"Have you seen this before?" he asked Carol then.

"No, I don't think so...what is it?" she replied, curious.

"A notebook full of handwritten notes...would you know if this could be Joe's handwriting?"

Carol examined the page the detective was showing her for a few moments. She recognised the scrawled writing style at once as being that of Joe. No-one else she knew wrote as badly as he had, like a child who'd never learnt.

"It looks very much like it," she told him. "He was rather bad at writing, as he never really studied much at school..."

"Thank you. Well, we'll leave you in peace now, and as soon as we've analysed this notebook we'll be in touch again."

"Okay...thank you..."

"Any other questions you need to ask?" he continued.

"Well, do you have any idea when I might be able to arrange a funeral for Joe? I think I owe him that, despite everything else..."

"I understand," the detective told her. "There will have to be a coroner's inquest once things have been sorted out, and when that is over, I think they'll release his body and so then you'll be able to make arrangements..."

"Thank you, detective..."

"Keep your spirits up anyway," he went on. "I've a feeling this little notebook is going to help us a lot with our enquiries, and then we can hopefully get the whole situation sorted out and dealt with..."

"What do you think about all that?" she asked Peter once they were alone again.

"Well, I think it's pretty clear now," Peter told her. "You are no longer of interest to them, and that's a very good thing in my mind. And with a bit of luck, that notebook might be the key to it all now. Are you quite sure it was his handwriting?"

"Yes, no-one else would write like that...and besides, who else would have left it where it was?"

"Did you manage to read any of it when he showed it to you?"

"No, not really...but I did see my name, so that's another proof I think..."

"Yes, definitely. Let's hope they'll find out a lot more as well..."

"Yes...it's strange, though, I never once saw Joe writing in it all the time he was here...it's like he kept a secret diary..."

"It seems like it..."

"Do you think they'd let me have it? I mean, once everything is settled..."

"I doubt it...it will be stored as evidence in the case...they might let you have a transcription though, if they deem it unimportant later on."

"I hope so. I really would like to know what Joe really thought about me and our relationship..."

"Yes, I can understand that, of course. But it might not be what you expect, and so my advice would be to forget about it..."

"Perhaps you're right. But still, it is curious, don't you think? And the way he hid it..."

"Obviously to stop you finding it and reading it, I should say."

"Of course...you're probably right there. All the same..."

Peter went back to work then, promising to call by later that evening. Carol, alone again, felt somewhat relieved, happy to get the chance to sit and review the whole affair without becoming upset or hysterical. Calmly, she tried to put all the pieces together, from the very start of meeting Joe, him moving in with her and supposedly working for her and with her, up to the final fiasco of the drugs and drink and the silences when he visibly detested her presence, if not the home she'd provided him with over several months.

Again, she tended to blame herself, even if by now she knew the truth. Love pardons anything, she felt certain of that, just as she'd been blinded by the enormous love he'd inspired in her, closing her eyes to all his weakness and bad intentions, as those around her now told her, including the police as they tried to establish the truth. All this swirled around her head endlessly, no matter what she tried to divert herself. TV, magazines, the radio, reading: nothing could stop the maelstrom of thought, and at times she felt as though she might be losing her mind. It would be a very difficult few days to follow, but she determined to see it through. She ached for Peter's return though, every time he left her alone. He was constantly on her mind, and she knew in herself the reason. But could she accept it ever again?

Chapter 42

Joe's black notebook proved to be a goldmine of information for the police, and D.I. Draycot asked himself if that had been Joe's intention, in case anything should happen to him, a kind of security guarantee, although it obviously hadn't worked in that sense. But for him, it facilitated his task enormously. It was filled with all manner of useful information: names and addresses, business objectives, Joe's own dealings and money-making, as well as passages about him living with Carol at her expense.

Working alongside the drug squad, who already had the gang under surveillance, he quickly established a pattern of what had happened, and why Joe had been shot. He'd written about the money and drugs he was skimming off the totals he should have rendered each week, and how the bosses had found out when someone squealed on him, and so he'd been issued with a final warning: pay it all back or face the direst of consequences, which in that world meant only one thing. That's when he'd no doubt helped himself to a big haul of both drugs and cash and tried to get away in Carol's car. That would explain the stuffed bag he'd carried with him on the last night at Carol's house.

But what was far more of interest to the police was the fact that he'd named every one of his associates and fellow dealers, as well as noting their addresses. The police couldn't believe their luck in a sense, as it made the following up of their enquiry one of the easiest they'd ever known.

A few days later, there took place a series of dawn raids across the town, and the whole gang was under lock and key before they knew what was happening. There was also a huge haul of drugs and cash, and so they were unable to deny the evidence of being involved, no matter how astute the crooked lawyers they hired might be. The evidence was overwhelming, and Joe's black notebook hammered the last nail into their fates. They also found a black holdall that matched the description Carol had given them, still filled with huge amounts of cash and drugs. If Joe's fingerprints and DNA were found to be on the bag, it was all the evidence the police would need.

If someone had shopped them, it couldn't have been Joe, as they well knew. But who, then? The police played on this ambiguity to their advantage, using the testimonies of one against another, until total chaos reigned throughout the custody cells. They all suspected one another of squealing to save their own skins, which D.I. Draycot had worked to achieve. It became almost child's play then for him to get the statements of each one separately, and then simply analyse and add up the details to discover the truth about who shot Joe, and for what reason.

A few days later, the apparent boss of the syndicate, Eric Carlyle, was charged with the first-degree murder of Joseph Fowler, with most of his acolytes being charged alongside him as accessories to the fact. Not one of them escaped charges of some kind: accessory to murder, drug trafficking, importing illegal substances, assault and battery, and a host of other minor offences that would make certain that they would all be off the streets for many long years to come. The large amount of drugs the police had confiscated also meant there would be fewer drugs on the streets for a while, and the raid and arrests would also put the fear of similar arrest into the other gangs operating in the area, which the police knew was a very good thing.

Carol followed all this with immense interest, reading reports in the local newspapers and listening to radio and TV bulletins. It was big news for the moment, and everyone seemed to be talking about it. Concerning Joe, she still couldn't fully accept that she would never see him again, although she knew she must. Harbouring feelings inside was not a good method for overcoming grief, or love, or anything else she might imagine she still felt. She feared sometimes for her own sanity, but fought back vigorously, knowing that if she succumbed, she would once again end up as her mother had, prostrate in mental wards and drugged to the hilt to stop any true feelings arising ever again. She didn't want that, she was certain.

Peter lived up to his name and became as a rock for her, always ready to pop round if she was down and try his best to lift her up. He knew deep down that he was in love with her and always had been. Now, with Joe gone, he felt the time was ripe for him to advance slowly towards a full relationship, slowly being the key word. If he rushed her off her feet now it would be catastrophic, and so he must bide his time. He was convinced his day would come.

EPILOGUE

When the date for the inquest had been announced, Peter advised Carol not to attend. He would go in her place if she wanted, and report back to her firsthand how it went and what was said. He knew she would be far too vulnerable and upset to sit through such tragic official parlances, and she thankfully agreed. She wanted it all to be over once and for all, and this was a first step in her mind. When she next spoke to Elizabeth, she told her what they had decided, and she agreed with them. Better to distance herself gradually and build up a new sense of life and freedom, and Peter was there for her whenever she needed a friend. Elizabeth had understood, more than she let on.

The coroner at the inquest announced that it was a straightforward case of first-degree murder, and the police had established and arrested all those culpable of committing such a wicked crime, so the inquest was merely a formality to ascertain and record the facts before a trial could take place. Peter attended as arranged, taking notes for Carol's benefit, although he was pleased that her name was never mentioned. D.I. Draycot was also in attendance, and when it was over and a verdict of death by murder, namely a gunshot wound to the back of the skull, was pronounced as the final verdict, he came over to speak with Peter.

"How is she bearing up?" he asked in a friendly tone.

"Not too badly," Peter replied. "I just thought it would be better for her not to be here today and have to relive it all again. She is still very upset and vulnerable, you understand?"

"Yes, of course. She's very lucky to have you close-by, I think…"

"Absolutely…we do go back quite some way, when I worked with her on her magazine…"

"Yes, I've seen all that…and I sincerely hope she will get her life back on route again quickly…"

"Me too…I think she's strong enough for that…but will she have to give evidence at the trial?"

"Hm, well, that's a tricky one for me to answer, you know. We won't call her as a witness, because everything we needed to know was written in that notebook we found at her house. Joe covered his back pretty well, and the others certainly weren't expecting that…but the defence might decide to call her, and then she'd have to turn up, I'm afraid, although I'm quite sure they won't. She didn't know any of them, and so what good would it do? It might even be worse for them in the end, if she told the court how they'd used and manipulated her through Joe, so I don't think she needs to worry on that score…"

"That's good to know. I'll tell her when I see her."

"Okay. Is there anything else I can help with?"

"Well, she would like to arrange a funeral service for Joe, but don't know when the body will be released…"

"Oh, that will be very soon now," the detective told him. "Now the coroner has signed the official documents, as soon as it's been registered, she'll be able to claim the body...a couple of days, I should say..."

"Ah, that will be a relief for her, I'm sure."

"Yes, I'm sure...she was in love with him, I gathered from Joe's notebook..."

"He wrote about her as well then?"

"Yes, but mostly as part of his long-term plans to inveigle his way into her life and take as much as he could from her in terms of money and other material things. He noted that she had an apartment in Spain that would be an ideal headquarters for the gang, as most of their stuff came via Spain, and he had managed to snatch the keys when he left. It wasn't a pleasant read to be honest...he was a bad person at heart, and in my opinion she's better off without him..."

"I agree...will she be able to get the notebook back when this is all over? She told me she'd like to read it."

"No, I'm afraid not, it will be part of the evidence to be archived in our system. I don't think it would do her good to read it, anyway..."

"That's all right then. I'll let her know..."

"Okay, Mr. Tierney...and if ever you need any advice about anything, feel free to get in touch with me..."

"Okay, thank you, detective..."

They shook hands and went their separate ways. Peter hurried back to Carol to give her an account of the inquest, and to relieve her of some of her anxious doubts and questions. She listened in silence, feeling mortified about it all, especially when the cause of death had been mentioned. A gunshot wound to the back of the head: true gangster style, as the coroner had pronounced solemnly. That made her weep, but not hysterically. She seemed to have come to terms with everything that had happened and was ready to move on.

"The good news is that the body will be released in a day or two, so you'll be able to arrange a funeral if you still want to…"

"Ah, that is good news…I would like to make sure he's laid to rest somewhere calm and peaceful…I feel I owe him that much at least…"

"Of course…and I'll help all I can…"

"Oh, Peter…what would I do without you?"

"Well, that works both ways, you know, Carol…" he told her with a wry smile.

She understood what he meant and curled up against him on the sofa.

***

Ten days later, Joe's funeral service took place at the local crematorium. Elizabeth came up to support Carol, and it was a solemn affair. Peter had taken care of all the arrangements, sparing Carol that morbid side of it all. He was to be cremated, and his ashes buried in the gardens surrounding the crematorium. To their mutual surprise, two of the nuns from the convent attended. That pleased Carol, who knew how Joe had been almost happy sometimes while at the children's home. Elizabeth was also happy to see them. There but for fortune, she could see herself in that same role, she thought to herself.

It was a simple and solemn service, quickly dispatched, and as the coffin disappeared behind the curtains Carol couldn't control her emotions, and sobbed loudly and openly in the near-empty chapel of rest.

"Goodbye, my Joe," she sobbed. "I did love you with all my heart, and I'll never forget you, my darling..."

***

When Carol checked her finances as she reserved Joe's funeral arrangements, she was horrified to learn that her regular accounts were almost depleted. For some time now she hadn't looked at her accounts, with her drug addiction and all the rest of Joe's scheming making her indifferent to normal life. But now she discovered that he had literally taken thousands from her accounts, having wheedled her cards and pin numbers from her while still professing his love for her, and she, naively, hadn't even noticed. Ditto with the car, of course, which she had now recovered from the police.

Peter advised her to talk with the bank manager, and the police, and to try to recover at least part of her money, but she was loath to do so. She again felt it was all her own fault, and she had no desire to blacken Joe's name any further. She alone must accept the consequences of her own blind stupidity.

"I'll just have to start work again," she decided. "I did it once, and I know I can do it again…"

"Well, that's a good idea," Peter told her. "But it won't be easy…"

"It doesn't matter. I can feel it inside, and I know Joe would be sorry now if he came back and saw what he did to me…"

"You still have feelings for him, then?"

"Yes, in a way…but not like before, so don't worry…I'm happy that you are near me now as well, and that's what counts most. Money can always be found, but not true feelings…"

Peter looked into her eyes as she spoke, and he felt all the depth and meaning she'd intended him to. That pleased him enormously.

"Well, maybe you're right, so, let's begin on the new magazine, shall we…?"

"Oh, Peter, do you really mean that?" she asked, incredulous.

"Yes, I do…I wouldn't be able to do anything full time, of course, not with my own business taking up so much of my time, but I could pitch in when you need me, and I do have the experience, remember…"

She laughed then, and that lit up Peter's face. To see her laugh openly once again, as in previous times. He thanked his lucky stars one more for allowing him to be so close to this woman, abused and half-broken, yet still the kind and caring woman he had fallen in love with from the start.

"Okay, you're hired again, Mr. Tierney!" she chuckled, and he knew then that he was nearing his own goals.

***

The trial took place six months later. Carol hadn't been called to give evidence, which was a huge relief. She knew she wouldn't have been able to stand up in Court and speak about her life with Joe, and all that had ensued. But she did attend on the day of sentencing, accompanied by Peter, because she wanted to see the people who had been responsible for his killing and look them in the eyes.

The leader of the gang, Eric Carlyle, was given a life sentence, with a minimum term of 41 years before he could be considered for parole. The rest of the gang received sentences of between 11 and 20 years, putting them out of circulation for the good of the community, as the judge announced solemnly.

Carol stared intensely at Eric Carlyle throughout the brief hearing and felt sad at not seeing any sign of regret or sorrow in his face for what he had done. He stood there calmly while the judge harangued him about his terrible crimes and greed, and then it was all over. They were led away, and Carol felt as though a great weight had been lifted from her shoulders. They would pay for what they had done to Joe, and that was enough for her now. No forgiveness at all from her. It was time to bury it all and move on.

***

Over the next year or so, things gradually returned to normal in Carol's life. She worked on the magazine again and soon had it up and running, not quite as glitzy as the previous issues but with a steady turnover of faithful readers who kept it afloat. Peter did all he could to help while Elizabeth lent a hand as well, as both were anxious to see Carol happy again and living a normal life.

She was seeing a lot more of Peter during this time, and she felt her love for him slowly rekindling as she moved further away from her past life with Joe. She did love Peter; she was certain of that now and felt a deep gratitude for how he had stood by her through thick and thin.

Now, he was still there at her side, often taking her out for meals and helping to get the magazine issues ready. They also started going away for camping weekends when Peter's children stayed with him, and she gradually looked upon them as part of her family, the children she would never have, but without sadness. They were bright children, always warm and friendly towards her, and Peter was a good father, as she soon saw. It was a happy time for all of them.

And then one evening, when they were alone together in a very chic restaurant/piano-bar named **'Candelabra & Ivory Keys'**, Peter suddenly took hold of her hand, much to her surprise.

"Carol," he began, a little flustered. "Can I ask you a question?"

"Why, yes, of course you can. What is it?"

"Will you marry me?"

Carol was completely floored by this, struck speechless, so unexpected was it. The pianist/vocalist was playing an old Ella Fitzgerald classic song, *'Paper Moon',* and it seemed so fitting at the time, as they would both recall in the future. Especially the line:

'But it wouldn't be make-believe, if you believe in me...'

"Oh, Peter...are you serious...?" Carol gasped, trying to control her emotions.

"I've never been more serious in all my life," he replied.

She looked deeply into his eyes, and saw the sincerity written clearly in his loving glance. How could she possibly resist?

"Then yes, Peter, I will marry you..."

And on that evening, it appeared that Carol's whole future had been decided once and for all. They made an exception to their rule about alcohol, and ordered a demi-bottle of champagne, with which they toasted each other. The whole restaurant, all eyes fixed upon them, erupted into a thunder of applause and cheering, and Carol realised that Peter had planned this whole thing in advance.

She was speechless with happiness now, not sorrow and pain, and that was such a new thing for her to experience again, like the taste of something exquisite she had eaten long ago as a child and ever since had been looking for it; a taste that had remained hidden in her soul ever since, waiting for the day it might show itself again. That evening was the day. Overwhelmed, her tears of joy streamed down her face, and she laughed properly for the first time in a very long time.

"I will no longer fight against my destiny..." she vowed that same night, and she held true to that for the remainder of her life, finding happiness and fulfilment with Peter, who loved her as no-one else ever had.

About the author

Dennis Meredith came to writing very late in his life. Full details of that life can be found in the two volumes of the autobiography he wrote in his first attempts at book writing: **MY LIFE – THE WAY I SEE IT** and **FROM STREET URCHIN TO MAYOR.** A fascinating story that begins in the bombed ruins of East London after WW11 and his endless struggles against poverty and neglect while growing up, and then takes him through countless adventures and situations to eventually become Mayor of Northampton. Quite an achievement.

But what comes through in his writing is the constant wave of optimism, even when faced with the direst of problems, and a determination to pull himself up and a faith in the people he encounters and works with to better his own position.

His following books, **THROUGH THE WINDOW,** and now this one, **VIRTUE, DIVINITY, DESTINY,** are both works of fiction, although stamped throughout with the author's traits and experiences, which transform themselves to become his first tentative experiments at storytelling. Struggling with dyslexia, which has dogged him from childhood, he has made a brave and strong effort to write with his heart and soul, and the fact that these four books now exist are a great accomplishment.

The adage tells us that everyone has a book inside them. Dennis has now written four. Surely that tells us also that the effort is worthwhile, and that these four books are waiting to be read.

It is the least we can do to encourage him to continue writing.

Printed in Dunstable, United Kingdom